I0657669

STRANGERS
IN MY MIND

STRANGERS IN MY MIND

STORIES OF CHARACTERS WHO INVADED THE MIND OF

DAVID PORTEOUS

The New Atlantian Library

THE NEW ATLANTIAN LIBRARY

is an imprint of
ABSOLUTELY AMAZING eBOOKS

Published by Whiz Bang LLC, 926 Truman Avenue, Key West, Florida 33040, USA.

Strangers In My Mind copyright © 2017 by David Porteous. Electronic compilation/ paperback edition copyright © 2017 by Whiz Bang LLC. Cover photograph by Jean Schweibish

All rights reserved. No part of this book may be reproduced, scanned, or transmitted in any form or by any means, electronic or mechanical, including photocopying, recording, or any information storage and retrieval system, without permission in writing from the publisher. Please do not participate in or encourage piracy of copyrighted materials in violation of the author's rights. Purchase only authorized ebook editions.

This is a work of fiction. Names, characters, places, and incidents either are the product of the author's imagination or are used fictitiously, and any resemblance to actual persons, living or dead, businesses, companies, events, or locales is entirely coincidental. While the author has made every effort to provide accurate information at the time of publication, neither the publisher nor the author assumes any responsibility for errors, or for changes that occur after publication. Further, the publisher does not have any control over and does not assume any responsibility for author or third-party websites or their contents. How the ebook displays on a given reader is beyond the publisher's control.

For information contact:
Publisher@AbsolutelyAmazingEbooks.com
ISBN-13: 978-1945772429 (The New Atlantian Library)
ISBN-10: 1945772425

For my scattered surviving family,
friends, adored wives and lovers,
I portray slivers of nuances of us
within this book's fictional folk.

- Dave P.

STRANGERS IN MY MIND

THOSE STRANGERS ...

MIND YOU...

These stories aren't autobiographical, but they and their characters reveal my views of life. However, they came to me with personalities and situations formed as mind-invaders because their presences prevented me from working on other projects; they refused to go until I wrote their stories. An example of many inspirations for people's motives... Hearing hunters' guns in fields near a school, I felt parents' fears of a shot hitting a kid, and in came Bart Novak in *What Matters*. Although the first 19 stories are fiction, my last offering is a wry essay on a fiction writer's life of mind-invading craziness.

I chose to offer tales whose characters have diverse story-telling styles or cultural forces, and some stories echo others to expand those themes. I haven't defined their settings – New York, Sydney, Shanghai or Paris is irrelevant to people dealing with life's universal issues. Some Short Story writers describe scenes in detail, and novelists voluminously explain plots, but I write about people and offer them for your mind to see how you want them to be. Few of you will '*see*' my fictional folk exactly the same, but you can all use my focus on their humanity to understand them. I hope you will enhance the lives your mind has helped to create by imagining their back-stories from the clues my tales provide.

Thanks for being adventurous readers – I enjoyed compiling this offering for you, and I welcome your feedback...

J. David Porteous
HuntAndPeckDave@Optimum.net

i

WORLD WAR THREE

They'd been waging World War Three for as long as he could remember; not a day passed without the sounds of sniping or spiteful attacks. Not physically, that was beyond their pales, but the crippling character assassinations that maim generations of families. He'd deduced from all they yelled at each other that they had had been fighting forever, so couldn't imagine why they married after identifying each other's pain thresholds.

As an only child, his survival amid their war was never easy. He was the grenade they'd lob into battle to inflict more pain than the usual abusive volley. It hurt him more than the intended victim, and the pain lasted to his twenties, spawning cynicism about relationships and a need for bulwarks against his parents. Although he now kept most of it at bay, he still got unwillingly conscripted into serving as an ally.

He knew they loved him in their ways, but not why they used him as a weapon, or why he had to be an innocent victim in the minefields they set. As he tried to ignore their current clash, he thought about how one would list the other's flaws and add "the boy agrees". It sent the wounded one to him for an explanation. He'd offer a diplomatic truth that always got adapted to the grenade of: "The boy says you're a liar." He then had to pacify the other warrior until a new battlefield formed, and hope it would be un suitable for grenade-lobbing.

He hated the sneering attacks on unforgiveable defects in one's family and return barrages at the other's, all as deeply wounding personal invective that left life-long scars. Being a grenade in these battles had destroyed respect for his parents and forced retreat to introspection that hindered his growth as a man. He resented being unable to bond them with pride in him; he was too insecure to excel in a career, or to sustain relationships with women who acted willing to share his life, but not to help him escape from it. He still lived at home, hating it, but seeing no option that he could manage.

He became aware of a silence that would lead to one of the combatants invading his room with an explosive array of grievances. These were treacherously tough encounters. His mother came armed with tearful self-rebuke for ignoring her mother's warnings, and pathetic blackmail to get his support for her next foray against 'the swine'. His father's arsenal had only doleful lectures on the folly of marrying, and wounding shots at him for not being the caliber of son other men have.

After truly cruel battles, his father sometimes hit him. Not that he got badly hurt; at worst he had to excuse a cut or bruise plausibly, and he was adept at that. He knew his father was venting pent-up fury on him, which was preferable to his mother being hit. He'd come to see that those physical attacks symbolized his father's frustration with a life that had never matched his dreams. Not that his mother's matched hers.

He had some sympathy for his father, who was derided as a disgusting drunk whether he had one beer or ten. With that home-coming greeting, it was reasonable that his father chose to have more than one and deserve to participate in the ensuing conflict. No amount of protestations about how few beers he had consumed saved his father; a single beer drunk equaled a real and repulsive drunk to his mother.

Her less evident need for war was also explicable. She was the child of a genteel family still embracing aspirations for that life in a marriage to working class reality. Her attacks' fuel flowed from a well of hostility about life with a class enemy, refined by resentment of his father's not appreciating the elegance she brought to family life. His parents were as different as war and peace, and why neither had seen that in time to avoid a life of conflict never ceased to amaze him.

The door swung open so fiercely that papers on his desk scattered. His father stood there, red-faced and fuming from the battle and the beers before it. There seemed no alternative to making evasive small talk at times like this, so he tried: "Hi, dad. Dinner ready?"

"You'd have to ask your mother. She's got the answer for every-fucken-thing!"

As his father marched in and sat on the bed in moody silence, he anticipated another rambling lecture on woman being man's natural enemy. But his honed instincts prickled when he saw in the blotchy face that something more volatile was about to surface, though he saw it too late.

"What's this shit? Brought work home? You better be getting extra pay for it!" The tone and accompanying sneer were clearly intended to provoke an argument.

He gathered up his papers to stall so his voice could be calm. "No... Just reviewing some things I've written. Marking them for edits to do in the computer, but–"

His father erupted: "Fucken poems again? Jesus... Never thought a son of mine would get into that fairy shit!"

Ignoring the assault, he imagined an impenetrable wall against barrages. He'd escaped almost unscathed from prior battles by mentally ridiculing their weapons as 'the slings and arrows of outrageous parents', but now he had to review this new development. Was he in his father's firing line from siding with his mother too often, or had she again called him an ally without his consent? Could attacks on his poetry be to camouflage

3

disdain for his membership of the local Drama Society? His father said that only gay men liked stage shows, so could he see a son's involvement as a slur on his own masculinity? Could his father really believe he is gay, a ludicrous word to apply to anyone in that house? Its different meanings amused him too much to prevent a smile tilting his lips.

"Think it's funny? I'm trying to stop you turning out fag!" His father's tone held real concern and beer-befuddled anger.

This salvo from the kitchen saved him from having to answer: "Dinner's ready! Get in here!"

As his father silently rose and trooped into the hall, his thoughts halted him. He was not only a perpetual victim of their war; his only safe zone could be wrecked by it. If the Drama Society was to be targeted in battles, or a weapon in them, he would never know a peaceful retreat to a place where everyone tried to be uplifting. He began to dread what the future would hold, and the fact that it could be just a continuation of what he had.

LIGHTING UP A ROOM

What can I tell you about The Silver Cat Trading Company? I worked there for six years before the fire, seeing it from its peak to ashes, so to speak. But are you also asking me about the Silver Cat's owner, who called herself Cat Silver?

Yes, Charlize, to tell her company's story, I need hers. Starting with her name. Do you know why she used it? All I could dig up is vague and seems full of contradictions.

No surprise. That lady created herself in layers so she could show whoever she wanted to be, or hide her real self. Anyhow, if you're recording now, I'm ready to go. But you should call me Charlotte. It's my real name. Being called Charlotte the harlot was too much to take, even for me.

I can see that. And I am recording, but though that 'show or hide' thing about her is intriguing, I should start at the beginning. When was that, and why did she call herself and her business those names?

She'd say Catalina DaSilva is a Portuguese name, but not if it's her family's or husband's name. Neither is true. Her parents were Italian, and she told me she'd never married. All I know is the name and her hair were the basis of the business name. But that all started... Well, decades ago.

Wait. Her hair? How does that come into any of this?

Her hair is the same...it went gray in her twenties. She couldn't afford to dye it, so that hair became as distinctive as her gorgeous face and double-D boobs. Silver hair gave her a sort of cute dominatrix look. And she had that smile. If any smiles light up a room, hers did. It was luminous, and not fake. Her looks and the personality she let the world see got instant attention, but her smile was totally captivating.

Fine, but we've gotten off the name. You said she was really Italian?

Her parents. She was born here, sixty-odd years ago. Not that you'd know by how she looked, even at the end with that vile illness. In makeup and wigs, she still looked great. Forty, tops. No makeup exposed her papery skin, but that wasn't just age. All the meds took a toll, so only the working girls at Silver Cat Trading saw her without make up. She'd talk to girls she liked, like me, and made us her friends.

What's her real family name...and why not use it?

Off the record... It was Biannalli. She changed it to Bean after college. So she's Belinda Bean, nicknamed Bindi at times... Another layer that led your research to contradictions. It's how she wanted it. Who'd guess Catalina DaSilva was really Bindi or Belinda Bean, who was originally named Biannalli?

Explains a bit. But not why. What was wrong with being Belinda Bean? And why can't I use it?

She couldn't let it lead to Biannalli. Her folks were old fashioned middle class Italians. Family honor was everything. Cat couldn't let journalists near them. She distrusted the media, and despised any who wrote stuff she'd made up to show they'd researched her. Actually, privately it cracked her up.

So - what? Her parents knew nothing about her and her business? Or all her wealth?

Only that she paid for their ritzy retirement village life, and never talked about her work. She told me her Belinda life outside Silver Cat Trading was private. To understand that, try seeing her as Barnum and Bailey. Cat Silver-Barnum, promoter, or Belinda Bean-Bailey,

6

businesswoman. Belinda's fabulous smile showed her security in who she was. Cat's smile was a promoter's act... and brilliant, but the entrepreneur's smile was so serene it sparkled... She was a success.

But how successful? If she couldn't afford to dye her hair in her twenties, how and when did she get so rich?

It's easiest to start where she was, financially, when Silver Cat Trading burned down, then go back to how it began. You've seen photos of the Victorian mansion that housed the business? The company name on its title was buried in amongst legal jargon about Holding Companies, but the houses each side of it had Belinda Bean's name on their title deeds.

She owned them too? Jesus! Buying all three must have cost her a fortune in that part of town!

She said the renovations, legal fees and bribes cost more. On the left was her home...the other a Boarding House where her girls rented rooms. I lived there, and it was great. No need to clean, cook, or even make your own bed. But no men allowed. Take one to your room and you're out the next day. No home, no job, and no argument about it.

It's hard to imagine someone like Cat making a rule that... Well, extreme.

Belinda the businesswoman did it to protect her assets. So we're back to her wealth and three Victorian mansions she spent millions to buy and renovate... The business had five work floors, including the basement dungeon. Yet Belinda graduated as a Pharmacist with a student loan debt too high for her to buy a share or partnership in a drug store. She had to make her start by working for some dude who owned a store.

Fine, I get it – huge contrast from then to the end. But how did she get there?

She said she'd have stayed a Pharmacist, saving to

buy a partnership, but she fell pregnant. Her Catholic boyfriend said no abortion, but left when she was six months gone, too late for it. So Biannalli became Bean, and unmarried mother Bindi had to take her baby to work...her father didn't let her mother mind a bastard in his home! Imagine...a lovely young woman with a baby, graying hair, and a father who didn't let her mom help her! Worse, the boy is autistic, and doctors then didn't understand it like they do now. She struggled, paying for his expensive experimental treatments from only a weekly wage.

And, so the only way she could get beyond that was to become Cat Silver?

Yep...on her back. Cuties can choose their clients, so after taking her baby to work all day, she'd take men at home. She soon made more at night than days, so she left the drug store to do lunch and happy hour trade at clubs. She learned to be choosier... she could charge more, and get classier trade. Some men have fantasies of older women... even their mother or grandma, and they all loved her silver hair. That's what led to Belinda Bean becoming Catalina DaSilva, and earning enough to rent rooms and hire pretty girls to work for her.

And so The Silver Cat Trading Company became a business name?

Yes, owned by Holding Companies her Accountant set up over the years to be what she called a 'too-dense mess for the tax boys'. In the last year, I'd see him at her home, and though she was ill and sixty, they didn't spend all their time foxing the tax boys. That's just between us... don't use it. But twenty-five years ago she was able to buy those old mansions to put her life and business in them. That's when Silver Cat Trading came to life.

It's a strange name for a brothel, though. Why a trading company?

Belinda saw it as a gentlemen's lounge, where they traded money for indulgent luxuries. You can smile, but we girls had to meet standards for looks, health, how we spoke, and our ability to be any man's fantasy. Our private lounge had TVs and books, plus racks of costumes and makeup mirrors for the fantasy acts. We didn't see ourselves as brothel babes, but entertainers with sex in our act if men wanted it. Yes, if. Some just drank and talked to us, and often left as big a tip as the men who came to play.

Really, Charlotte? Can you give me some idea of that? Like, how big were those tips?

You can't use it, but my best was a thousand bucks. Full service, of course. But once we had six guys from Ohio, of all hick places, and each gave me five hundred. Three grand in tips! Plus my split of the action money from Belinda. So, yeah, we got big, big money! But, of course, Belinda made much, much more.

Let's get back to her and her 'gentlemen's lounge'. I know it was highly profitable, but can you give me examples of how she was a smart businesswoman?

You have to start by knowing that she would have retired long ago if not for her boy, Bobby. He still lives in her home, but she knew she'd always have to support him, so she set out to get rich for that. And when she got her diagnosis and knew she might not be here for his fortieth birthday, that business brain of hers kicked in to suck up every buck she could for him.

Before we get to that – seeing you've touched on her illness again, can you tell me what she had? There are rumors, but I'd like facts. I assume you know them.

Sure. She floated the rumors to protect Cat's image as The Silver Cat's face to let her Belinda side protect Bobby. They're two sides of one person, with Belinda as the planner protecting the Cat side. It seems crazy when I say it out loud, but Belinda did whatever she had to so she'd have money for Bobby. That included an almost life-long act as Cat Silver.

But the rumors say she had some sort of cancer, right?

Starting those rumors was genius. No one likes to talk about cancer, and it's so common people accepted Cat got it. The business we're in, people said uterine, cervical... or throat from head-bobbing. But she tested HIV positive, saw it as AIDS, and kept it secret so men didn't see her girls as death traps and stay away. Again, see Belinda, not Cat, who had to think of Bobby more after hearing she was on borrowed time. But... I'll give you two reasons why your story can't even hint about AIDS. After her diagnosis, we all had to have regular tests. Belinda hated paying for them, but insisted. Now, as some girls escaped the fire and are still working, if you link AIDS to Cat it could ruin them – their names were all over the news. Got it?

Sure. They tested clean...and two, let them move on.

No, that's all one reason. And if you print any of it, some of Cat's friends will be inclined to find you and bust your bones. Or worse.

You're not seriously trying to threaten me into putting a lid on that news?

No. I'm stuck in this Burn Unit for months of repair and rehab, but though I was Belinda's friend and am friends with girls who escaped the fire, I just gave you good advice. If you choose to ignore it... Well, don't. Now, let's move on.

What? As if I didn't get that 'advice'?

Sure. I told you not to use it, and why. Like when I said don't report Belinda and her Accountant were romping. I'm not saying you'd be hurt for exposing that now, but I've let you know that there's a real risk of some guys getting nasty if you even hint that Cat had AIDS. So, do we continue?

I suppose. We've come this far. So what's another business example?

The best was arranging to buy herself out of her own business. It actually began before the HIV test. She put girls who'd been with her for ten years on a profit sharing plan. How it worked was they'd get back some profit Belinda made on their work, but had to invest it in Silver Cat Trading stock. Cat sold the business bit by bit. I joined too late to get in, but twenty girls had the dough to buy the business and its building... Well, had enough for a big deposit that let them get a mortgage for the rest.

If you weren't in on the deal, how do you know these details about it?

I told you we hung out in the private lounge, and it was all we talked about in that last year. The girls were too excited to keep anything secret! Until planning the farewell party for Belinda got to be the main top topic.

I heard she was just going to be on the Board...no?

The girls would run it as a Holding Company she'd set up...Cat House Board, d-b-a Silver Cat Trading Co. Belinda had a friend, a private equity banker, get the girls' mortgage. She'd be a consultant... If her health let her. She was getting unsteady... and struggled to get up from a chair. But the deal gave Bobby income from the Boarding House, while running the home and staff she hired for him were funded by all she'd made, including the sale, and her life insurance pay out. She told the girls not to say what they'd paid, but I heard it was four million deposit, with an eight million mortgage.

That is a good businesswoman! Great example, thanks. So I take it that the party was less a farewell from the trade and more a tribute to her...right?

No, 'thanks' for all she'd done for us. We expected her to be next door, popping in for a chat, so we wanted it perfect for her. But Belinda insisted on picking out the decorations, and fussed about what they were made of. Well, we had all made big bucks working for her, so we bought whatever she wanted to make our lounge a harem fantasy...lacy drapes, ostrich feather fans, gold plates, crystal Champagne flutes... all that. We wanted to indulge Belinda with the sort of luxuries that she'd provided for years, and we set the head table on a dais so she could see everyone.

Apart from the few we know died in the fire, there are rumors of other celebrities and politicians there. Can you give me some names? Any real big-shots?

Ah... Everyone made an anonymous entrance in a gold mask. Not that the masks hid them long...we'd been up close and personal, but I can't give names to a journalist. I have enough trouble with skin grafts and rehab to risk angering big-shots who don't live on the legal side of life. Know what I'm saying?

Sure...okay. So let's cut to the chase. Describe how the night ended...your view of it.

So picture that room... White tablecloths with gold cutlery, plates, goblets and big flower arrangements, a sextet in a corner by a dance floor. Everyone dressed up and wearing gold masks with feathers trimming the women's and satin turbans on the men's... Non-stop Veuve Clicquot. Got it?

'Over the top' went over the top, extravagantly.

I told you we didn't chintz on a thing. So picture Belinda at the head table with her closest friends – yes, one is her Accountant, looking at people who'd made her rich. Most knew her as Catalina DaSilva, the alias she wants to live on as Belinda Biannalli-Bean lives in anonymity. She liked her alias being the figurehead of the company she'd sold to get out of the game and its risks so Bobby can have life's most indulgent luxury... Wanting for nothing.

What really happened that night? No one has been

prepared to provide much in the way of details. Even the Police report was... Understated, to say the least.

You don't need to be Einstein to figure out why. All I can tell you is what I heard from girls who visit me in here...they'd heard Belinda felt ill. I didn't notice, but maybe someone at her table mentioned it. What I know is, when she didn't feel as bubbly as her Cat persona had to be, she'd pop extra pain-killer meds so she could do her Cat act. If she did it to be up for the party, she shouldn't have had a drink. But she loved Champagne. Still, it was her exit from the world of sex – figuratively, by then, so she did what she pleased, and one thing was to thank her guests. Belinda tapped a fork on a glass, but only a few heard, so friends clinked on Champagne flutes, calling out: 'Speech, speech!'

She was, after all, our guest of honor, so the voices soon stopped, all eyes went to her, and everyone's fork was clinking. Word was out that she'd wanted to retire to a symbolic role at the company, and now her health had forced that. Some of us knew better, but we looked at our friend at the head table on the dais, ready to see her however she wanted to be that night.

When the clinking ended she stood, without help that I saw, and looked about, shining her famous smile on all who'd come to share her big night. And then... as best I can remember, she lifted her champagne flute. Now I'm damn positive that glass didn't even touch the candelabra on the table in front of her, but... Well, without any apparent cause, it fell over and instantly set alight the huge floral centerpiece. The last thing I remember is Belinda calmly continuing to smile as the whole fucking room seemed to just burst into flames.

HOW IT'S DONE

The diCabrio Winery's cool cellar heated up as a row between the family's patriarch and scion flared with fuming obstinacy. Niccolo diCabrio Senior's scowl told his son to drop the topic, but Nicco Junior merely paused until his sister Carmella turned on a spotlight over the tasting bar where the men stood. When she sat on a nearby bar stool, he continued speaking.

"She's your best son for the job, Papa. Claudio's not up to it, and Cesare would spend every day sampling until there's no wine to sell. Carmella is all you have, and you know how well she helped me here while you were so ill."

"You are a fool! Who could respect our Winery if they know a girl is running it? No! You must carry on our business as you do my name. It's how we diCabrios have always done it."

"Respecting tradition is fine, Papa, but Carmella also deserves your respect. She's the smartest of us, and at thirty-one is no girl! She overcame a lot to get so well educated, and you know it. You must put her in charge here. Must!"

The old man smiled at his daughter to calm any girly reaction to being discussed as if she wasn't there; her iciness made him flinch. He then saw Nicco's hard eyes as proof that his children were heartless monsters, and what Nicco had said finally hit home. "She's all I have? What will you be doing? I'll tell you! Doing what I've groomed you to do!"

Nicco's eyes rolled, mostly to ignore his father's smirk. "You won't like my answers, Papa. Sit down, and stay calm. Doc Zheng said you can't take any stress."

As Niccolo eased back onto a stool, Nicco saw six months' erosion of a once-robust man. He knew to let his father speak first, and feigned the expression of a son awaiting words of wisdom.

"I won't talk with her here, Nicco. Get her out"

"Carmella stays. If you have something to say that's not your usual rubbish about women in business, spit it out."

"Don't take that tone with me, boy! I won't let her hear my plans for a future that I don't want her to be a part of!"

"Jesus, Papa! Why won't you tell me why?"

"How in good God's name can a son of mine be too stupid to see a dummy can't run diCabrio Winery?"

Decades of repressed frustration ignited in Nicco's voice. "She's no dummy! You know she understands everything, and you must see that my future is at the restaurant Maria and I bought, so you have to let Carmella look after you and this biz!"

"I say your place is here! You can't leave all our family built - and me! - in that girl's hands."

As the old man struggled to stand, Nicco saw panic in his eyes. "Sit down, Papa! Your face is going red... No, purple!"

Niccolo couldn't hide being glad to flop back, but his voice was harsh. "What? Give a girl my life's work while you go off to play in a city restaurant? I'm to just accept that? No, boy, it would be the death of me!"

Carmella rose and came to stroke her father's hair. It looked like the act of a loving daughter, but Nicco knew her imperfection fueled their father's bitterness that had always made life miserable for her and her twin brother, Claudio. Neither of the twins had any love left for the old man.

"Listen to me, Nicco! Your mind's wandering."

"Only to Doc Zheng's advice to stay calm or your

next heart attack will kill you. You don't heed him, but hear this... I can't care if leaving to do something for my family triggers that attack. So the bottom line for the business is... I'm going, so if Carmella doesn't run it, it's your stupidity that'll kill you."

Niccolo shook off Carmella and roared: "So go! Don't stay to shame me like she does! But know that I won't let her meddle in how I want my business run!"

Nicco hissed: "You don't deserve her! She'll stay to care for you, who never even bothered to learn sign language to talk to her. Only a shitty father disrespects a daughter like that!"

Niccolo's attempt to speak failed, so Nicco said: "I told Carmella to come with Maria and me to enjoy a new life. But no. She'll stay for Claudio, the winery and you. In that order. The Power of Attorney you signed in hospital gave me control, and I would put Carmella in charge anyway, but it's happening early. Get used to it. We really don't care what you think."

A now gasping Niccolo again tried to stand, but fell back on the stool, his mouth gurgling, arms limp and head lolling. Carmella felt for a pulse, then shook her head. Surprised to see tears in her eyes, Nicco hugged her, but they maintained eye contact; it was how they communicated. He called out toward a distant door: "Henri! I need you in here. Now!"

The tall, trim figure of diCabrio's Cellar Master, Henri Thibou, ran in from a well-lit hall and peered at Nicco holding Carmella. He only then noticed his dead employer. "Mon Dieu! Le pauvre m'sieur Senior! Oh, mes ami, I am so sorry. What do I do, m'sieur Junior? Tell me."

"Call for an ambulance. Tell them no hurry. And call Doc Zheng. Tell him Papa had the heart attack he predicted, so I need him here. Then send our brothers to me. Okay?"

"If you call le Docteur while I find them is faster, non?"

"Jesus, Henri! We just lost our father! I need to be with my sister."

"Ah, oui, of course. Je vais...immédiatement."

As Henri left, Nicco turned Carmella away from a view of their father's body to say: "Nothing's changed. I'll sign everything over to you except for my Presiding Directorship and shares. You'll be Executive Director. Cesare'll blow up about it, but I can fix him. Now... can you face the mob that'll be in here soon?"

She nodded, and then hand-signed to cover their father's face. When Nicco took a soiled handkerchief from the old man's vest to drape over the dulling eyes, Carmella read his inner mirth and wagged a finger as if scolding a child. Both were smiling until they heard an ambulance's siren and heavy feet running in the hall. Their eyes agreed: Cesare's arrival should be met with grave expressions, which they had as their only sibling replica of Niccolo Senior lumbered in.

The bulky middle son stopped to mop his sweaty face and study the room. He didn't bother to ask Nicco what had happened as he went to his father's slumped form, but as his brother joined him, he growled: "What the fuck did you do? Choke him to shut him up? Looks like it! Neck's dark and puffed up. You're fucked, Nicco! You won't get away with this."

"Heart attack. Henri called Zheng and he'll confirm it. So I'll ignore what you just said."

"No need. You're still a shit for laying a snotty rag on his face!" Cesare lifted the offending cloth from the now sightlessly staring eyes. "Jesus! You didn't even..." He closed the eyelids and held them, saying: "Ah, Papa, I'm sorry you died with this shit here." His tone turned malicious. "So how'd you do it? Taunts? Kept doing it to get a do-it-yourself death?"

"Oh shut up! We were planning how to do things now

Papa's forced to retire, and the business is—"

Cesare snarled: "Business? Not if she was here! Papa would never allow it! You know I know that!"

"But you don't know everything, Cesare. Like, you didn't know Papa knew Maria and I will be living in the city so I can give all my time to our restaurant. I admit he wasn't happy about it, but he understood. Even said it's best with our kids in college there to keep the family together. Anyhow, we'd just agreed on the winery when he... Went. Peaceful. And fast. No suffering. Well, not much. Be glad of that. So—"

"So I'm in charge! Great! Everything will be done right for the first time in months!"

Nicco didn't correct Cesare because the ambulance crew arrived and he wanted to return to his sister, who had gone to greet Claudio. He told Cesare to see their father was handled respectfully, and went to the twins. Cesare's face flushed with pride, but that dissolved to show his paranoia about Nicco's motive in making him responsible for their father's body.

As always, Nicco was delighted by seeing the twins together; both were strikingly cute, as if their mother had the two girls she wanted. Claudio had always tried to hide being gay, and Carmella and Nicco did all they could to help him live as freely as family burdens would allow. To put him at ease now, Nicco said: "You're free at last, kid. Enjoy it. Be who and what you want to be."

Claudio offered a feeble smile. "I wish! You don't think Cesare will let me just swish off into the sunset, do you?"

"I do. When I tell him Carmella's in charge, he'll go so nuts he'll sell his shares to us. He won't stay with a *girl,,,* even his brainy sister!... head of a business he thinks is his. And if I'm not here to deflect attention from you, the idea of living with an openly gay brother would drive him even crazier. That bent brain he got from

Papa will think that if it's known the family has one homo, people may think he's one. That's so horrible to him that it'll be easy to get this ending best for us three."

Nicco's predictions came true, mostly. After just one quarrel about management, Cesare was impatient to sell his shares in diCabrio Winery; his siblings snapped them up. It didn't take him long to buy a vineyard, farther along the valley, and he began poaching diCabrio workers who he knew disliked working for women, especially a mute one who gave orders via an arrogant French Cellar Master. However, to balance that, it didn't take Carmella long to learn that she was almost as glad to see those employees go as she was to find that they were easily replaced.

Claudio began the long gender reassignment process, and diCabrio Winery was ultimately run by twin sisters and the always quiet one's husband, Henri. Gossip about that fed Cesare's smearing of his siblings, who remained blissfully sure that his alcoholic-in-denial obstinacy would ruin his new venture. They were wrong in that; Cesare had inherited a genetic love of wines and wine-making, and had learned all its skills, so his Casa di Cesare Estates prospered from its first vintage.

Nicco, Maria and their sons lived in a large, plush city apartment above the restaurant he called 'Papa's'. That name amazed friends who knew he had despised Niccolo Senior, but he always enjoyed explaining the pun in its full registered name, which was: 'Papa di Pesto Pasta'. While he was building it to a huge success, his sisters were luring coach loads of tasters and buyers to the diCabrio Winery, greatly boosting his profit share from it.

Nicco's pride in ridding his family's business of a brother who was a repugnant reminder of their father almost matched how he felt about freeing Claudio to be Claudia, and getting Henri to marry Carmella. But his greatest pride derived from being able to see himself as the ancient diCabrio family's most successful patron ever. It was an opinion shared by few people in the valley's wineries and wine merchants' offices, who were rumored to see his victories as pyrrhic. However, when such gossip got to Nicco in his city isolation, he could easily shrug-off all such derision and move on as if he hadn't heard, living proof that even the superficiality of his ego was impenetrable.

A VERSION

Veteran Homicide Squad Detective Bernard Cuneo spoke only to give directions as his new partner, Pietro Diversi, drove. Diversi didn't mind; he was in awe of how Cuneo found clues in seemingly unrelated items, and was learning just by watching Big Bernie work. He already knew that the gallows humor of most homicide detectives had no place at crime scenes with a man who makes a mission of quickly identifying each killer.

"That parking lot ends behind the diner-and- show place we want. Got it, Pete?"

Diversi nodded; he'd seen flashing lights coloring the foggy night, and spectators in the lit-up site's dim fringes. He was learning to dislike the ghouls who came out to gawk at bodies at one in the morning.

A tall uniformed Sergeant waved for them to stop and, as Diversi lowered his window, asked: "Is Bernie in there?"

"Of course I am. What've we got, Niemanis?"

Sergeant Niemanis peered into the car. "Hi, Bernie. Dude tried to mug the show's audience stragglers. Staff came out soon after, saw our vic in a pool of blood and called us."

Cuneo heaved his bulk out of the car, beckoned the Sergeant to him, and asked: "Our victim got any I-D?"

Niemanis chuckled. "Mugger is the vic, with lots of stolen I-Ds. But his photo's on the Driver's License of Ernst Rilke. Rilke's record is – was – as muscle for a gang in Sutherland."

Cuneo sounded impatient. "Who've I got? Talk to me."

Niemanis sagged. "Sorry. Fifteen-hour shift so far."

As empathy softened Cuneo's face, the Sergeant added:

"Truth is, Leila's pregnancy's due to pop, so I just don't need to be here."

Cuneo draped an arm around the lanky man. "So let's get you back to that lovely girl a-s-a-p. Give her a hug for me."

Their amity gave Diversi new insight to Cuneo, but he tried to refocus them with. "Those 'who've we got' details, Sergeant?"

"Oh, right. Jim Dawson, old guy who fought Rilke, is waiting for you in his car. That V-W Passat. Upset the mugger is dead because of what he did saving our one witness. She's Zoe Pierce. Looks like a kid, but her I-D says twenty-one."

Cuneo asked: "So how did he kill our mugger for her?"

"No one's sure. She cell videoed the four seconds long fight... can't see anything in the fog. I let her keep the phone to call home after I got her statement. She was shaky. Want to hear it?"

"Wait." Cuneo turned to tell Diversi: "Check our vic. See that nothing gets fucked up. This is smelling weird to me."

As Diversi left, Niemanis read the statement. After hearing it, Cuneo nodded and said: "Got it. Zoe Pierce. But what's your take on Jim Dawson? You said old."

"Seventy. Just traffic tickets...and he'd have to sit on Rilke to hurt him. He's as fat as you, Bernie. But lucky! Rilke died in that short fight... holding a Bowie knife! So you're right... Something's weird here. It all looks simple, but it can't be."

Cuneo asked: "Power fat, like Sumo wrestlers?"

Niemanis said. "We shook hands. Strong grip. Said he kept fit until his thirties, when a new job, salesman, kept him too busy for going to gyms. Want to see him?"

"Her. You know the drill. Stay back, say nothing."

Cuneo climbed up into an ambulance to where a frail young woman sat gazing at her phone. When she looked up, he said gently: "I'm Detective Cuneo, Zoe. I won't keep you long, then I'll have you driven home. Or is your car here?"

A trembling head shake stuck lank hair to her pale face.

"But you were in a parking lot. Shortcut home?" She looked confused, so he tried: "To meet someone?"

She managed to turn a timid nod into a vaguely nonchalant shrug.

"Who?" Getting only a dull-eyed stare in response, he said: "Relax, it can wait. I'll talk to the Sergeant you talked to, and be right back."

Cuneo led Niemanis out of Zoe's hearing. "Remind me what she said about a man here. Anything not in your notes?"

"When I asked if she saw only the old guy and the bad guy, she said a man was at the dumpster. I asked if she knew him, and she got sort of flustered. Said maybe it was just a shadow. I pushed as hard as I could, but she was... like, numb. I took it as shock... or fear. She's skinny, and Rilke's fucking massive."

Cuneo nodded. "Maybe, but I'd say dumpster guy's her dealer. Have someone look for weed, powder, pills, or any shit."

Niemanis chuckled. "Sure to find something. Deals go down here all the time. But drugs aren't involved in this."

"No, but I'll use whatever's found to scare more out of the kid. And now, what about our old guy? Did he see anyone else?"

"Nah. Said his eyes were on the guy going at Zoe with, and I quote, 'a big ass knife'. Want to see him now?"

"First I'll tell her she can go. She did get a medical check, right? And you've verified all the contact details in her statement?"

On getting Niemanis' nod, Cuneo returned to the

ambulance while the Sergeant sent an officer to the dumpster, with a reminder that all drugs found would have to be given to 'Big Bernie'. He then told his only female officer, Kathy Kelly, that she would be driving Zoe home, and to report everything that was said.

Cuneo left the ambulance, heading to the body instead of back to Niemanis, and calling: "She can go. For me, time to contemplate our corpse. Come over. What do we know here?"

After telling Officer Kelly "Go", Niemanis shone a light on the body. "See? Back looks like it's broken and a crushed throat that didn't bleed much... just a bit out through his mouth."

Cuneo beckoned Diversi away from listing items near the twisted corpse. "Pete, meet Ojars Niemanis, a mighty fine cop I'd like in our squad. Niemanis, Pietro Diversi." He dryly added: "You could be a squad team of funny names."

"Oyah?" Pete queried.

"O-j-a-r-s. My folks are Latvian. Pietro? Italian?"

Cuneo chuckled. "Teaming up already? Now, did Forensics do their thing? Did anyone touch the body? Do we know?"

Niemanis said: "Tim Diaz and I got here first. Met our prime pair, the theater's manager and two staff. More had left. I got their names. Just Jim, fighting, and the manager looking for a pulse, touched Rilke. When they found he was dead, old Jim made the others keep away from the crime scene for us."

"Did he, indeed?" Cuneo asked. "And the theater trio?"

"Gave statements, saw nothing, so I let them go."

Diversi reminded the Sergeant: "Forensics...?"

"They and their cameraman left before you came. Did all they could in the fog... back at dawn. The other ambulance with its lights off is their meat wagon for when we release the body. I sent Diaz to get tarpaulins to cover this area, and I'll leave him to guard it tonight."

Cuneo said: "Our kind of cop, eh Pete? So, you can both aim your lights on our badly bent Mister Rilke." He peered at the body. "Right handed. Pete...carefully pull up his sleeve."

After studying marks exposed by the lights, Cuneo had their beams directed at Rilke's throat, now a dent in a once-muscular neck. Pointing to the body's twisted spine, he told Diversi that it looked to have separated when it broke, and heard in response: "Hell of a fight!"

"Yep. Now, Niemanis, stop me if I go wrong. But first... Do we know why our old guy and girl were the last of the audience out?"

"Old Jim went to the can, and Zoe made phone calls."

"And here our fat old guy fights a stand-over thug." Cuneo pointed down. "So why isn't this him with a neck crushed like that? No, our unarmed old guy did this. It is really weird. Time to read me his statement."

Niemanis shone a light on his pad. "I got verbatim notes in my sort of shorthand. Jim said... 'I always let others go before I leave my seat. My bad knees slow me and them up, so I was last out and went to the men's room. Prostate, I leak a lot. When I got out–'"

"Hold it," Cuneo interjected. "His knees... medical problem?"

"In my notes... Ah! College Rugby fucked his knees. He played Squash – ritzy racquetball, most of his life, and said it's a knee-fucker, too. He had both replaced in his sixties, but the double knee op ended bad, and–"

Cuneo snapped: "Short answer's fake knees! And it's a bi-lateral op. So, we have a jock who ran to fat with age... It happens. Did he box or wrestle? Even fucking sword fight? Anything that might explain that damage to Rilke?"

"Maybe... He said he learned a style of Karate that's

called Kyokushinkai... and did it for twenty years."

Cuneo's eyes tightened. "Did you ask if he's a Black Belt?"

"Sure did," Niemanis said, still checking his notes. "Got it. Black Belt at twenty-three. Took up Karate at eighteen, so—"

"So he was still learning at thirty-eight. What's it tell us? He's strong, and knows how to do damage, Karate-style."

Diversi scoffed: "No, he did, half his life ago. Now he's a fake-knees-fatty of seventy. Maybe he could still kill Rilke, but in four seconds? Nah!"

Cuneo mused: "Could a Karate chop do this to a throat? Maybe. But, yeah, it's hard to see our old guy doing it in a few secs. Your thoughts?"

As Diversi shrugged, Niemanis said: "Can't blame Jim. If he had the skill once, maybe his weight behind a lucky blow could wreck our vic's throat. But do we charge him if he was just protecting a girl?" He added pensively: "Don't Black Belt guys have to register their hands as weapons? Is that true?"

Cuneo snorted. "He may have, fifty-odd years ago, but my issue is this... Even if perps die during crimes, families sometimes sue for damages. So knowing their guy's killer learned how to cause that death could help Rilke's." He paused to get the men's full attention. "So no loose ends if we write it up as a self-defense accident while saving the girl. And that's still 'if'... Got it?"

Niemanis said: "She said she didn't know who had come to help her. No ties, intent, or weapon. Must be self-defense."

Cuneo shrugged. "Back to the old guy's statement."

"So, this is after he left the men's room... 'I saw staff tidying up, and a few of the audience outside as I went to my car. Zoe was the only one I saw back here until that man came. I thought to meet her, but she looked back and I saw her fear, even in this light, so I hurried, best I can, at him. My only plan was to stall him till she got away, but he swung a big ass knife at me. After that it's all a blur. I think I grabbed his arm to stop the knife, but he must have fallen on me. I had to roll him away to get up.'"

Niemanis paused as a Police car arrived, then said: "It's Diaz with the tarps. Want more of Jim's statement, Bernie?"

"No, I'll ask him if he's remembered anything else."

Niemanis asked: "How will you handle him?"

"He fought a guy who's now dead, so as a killer. If you mean interview, you may be too young to know the saying 'you can catch more flies with honey than with vinegar'. Truer for nice guys, and as you see him as one, I'll take impartial Pete with me."

Niemanis walked off as Diversi asked: "So I do...?"

"Keep your eyes on his face, ears tuned for wrong notes, and your mouth shut. If I ask you anything, give me a straight answer."

As they arrived at the VW, a beefy, gray-haired man got out and had to steady himself, so Cuneo said: "No need to stand." After Dawson sat with his feet out of the car, Cuneo shook his hand. "I'm Detective Cuneo. Sorry I'm late getting to you, but before you go I need some answers while it's still fresh in your mind. Okay? Good powerful grip you have, by the way. Real good."

The compliment surprised Dawson. "Oh? Well, I was taught as a kid that a firm handshake shows your commitment to accepting people. But yes, I'm okay. Thanks for asking. Some aches, but I'm more pained by that young man being... You know."

"Aches? Zoe videoed all four-seconds of that fight. I'd have thought it wasn't enough time to start aching."

Dawson laughed. "But you aren't yet an age when everything causes aches, Mister... Detective Cuneo."

"You can call me Bernie, most people do."

"Call me Jim. Same reason. But, to explain... I didn't just laugh at age aches. It was hearing the young lady filmed that scuffle instead of getting to safety, as I'd intended. Kids! Phones are now their lives, eh?"

"Yeah," Cuneo agreed amiably. "But we have real lives to get back to, so let's hurry. First, though... Did medics check you? No harm done?"

"They reset a dislocated finger. Said it's probably from my fall... landed on my back, and it's bruising. Right knee is, too. I suppose that big guy fell on it. Who knows? But I'll be fine. I had to learn to live with pains long ago."

Cuneo sounded sympathetic. "Friends with fake knees say they're not made to even kneel on, let alone fall on. But... Is it okay for me to look at that knee?"

Dawson again showed surprise, but nodded, so Cuneo held up the pants for Diversi to shine his light on the knee. After studying it, Cuneo said: "It's swelling above the patella...kneecap, and bruising, Jim. Needs ice a-s-a-p. Hurting much?"

"As I said... I had to get used to crappy knees... Now I don't let myself notice."

"Hurt kneecap's odd from falling back, so maybe he did drop on it. But now... The Sergeant said you couldn't recall the scuffle, as you called it. Has anything come back to you?"

"Sorry, no. Well... It felt longer than just seconds, but did happen too fast for me to even know what was going on."

"So, instincts kicked in?" To Dawson's 'what else?' shrug, Cuneo said: "The Sergeant said you're a Karate Black Belt, and I'd have thought getting to that top level would program instinctive reactions. Yes?"

Dawson said patiently: "A Black Belt really starts your learning. It proves you know and can control the basics, but a Black Belt has ten levels, called Dans... and I knew only one Master who'd made it to a Tenth. But, yes. Karate programs instincts to react to whatever you face." He smiled. "All my instincts are rusty...I haven't trained for at least thirty years."

Cuneo smirked. "I hear you. I'm only forty-five and I feel rust forming. But it's time you got home to ice that knee. Always loose ends, so I'll get you to my office... or maybe I can come to you... Yes?"

Dawson said softly: "I'd prefer that. I don't drive much now. Knees stiffen-up if I sit too long without moving my legs. There's also the cost of gas. Now I'm retired on a fixed income, I have to choose carefully where to use what cash I have."

Cuneo's smirk resurfaced. "Like spending it on a dinner-show here?"

"I budget for two a year," Dawson said seriously, then he smiled ruefully. "T-V dinners alone at home are my real life."

Diversi got a second glimpse of his big partner's nature as Cuneo's expression melted with compassion. "It's late, Jim. You go now... I'll call if I need follow-up. Drive safely."

As Dawson drove off into the fog, waving to the Detectives, Cuneo asked: "So... Impressions, Pete?"

Diversi didn't hesitate. "Ojars is right. Seems a nice old guy with good values. I can see he was strong, and is tough to live in constant pain, but I can't see him deliberately killing Rilke. I heard no cover-up or excuse for anything, just regret that Rilke ended up dead. And you, Bernie?"

"Yeah, seems nice. Probably is. Let's be sure the area's secure, then go to the car's computer to alert the M-E's office that I'll be sending a preliminary report tonight with questions I'll need answers to tomorrow."

Niemanis heard that. "You doubt that it was just

accidental in a self-defense fight, Bernie? So you still think it's weird?"

Cuneo snapped: "Ojars...Pete...think! It looks like a truck hit this guy's back and neck. And yet before he swung a big ass knife at a nice old man, he was a huge, healthy thug. So, if we think of writing-off our thug's 'accident' as justice being served – which we may want, how we report this has to be too watertight to raise any questions. That means no charge, and no civil suit. Got it? So it also means... Yeah! I've got questions!"

Niemanis said: "I do too. Can the meat wagon take Rilke?" On Cuneo's nod, he signaled to the ambulance's driver, then asked: "What changed for Zoe? You let her go without using the drugs we found to make her talk."

"That can wait. She was a mess. I barely got her to look at me instead of at her gold-cased iPhone, and–"

"Gold iPhone?" Niemanis queried. "No, I tried to see Zoe's video on a red Samsung. I had Kathy Kelly check Zoe to be sure she could give a statement. And, of course, check for drugs...whatever. Kathy reported all she saw... No gold phone. Maybe Rilke dropped it in the fight, and Zoe saw that and got it later? We'd left her alone. How else?"

Cuneo shrugged. "And how important? But let's focus on what's left to do so we can get out of here."

~ ~ ~

Cuneo was in his office at 6:25 P.M. that same day, talking to Sergeant Niemanis by phone, as a link to an email from the Medical Examiner popped-up on his computer screen. Hoping it was about Rilke's autopsy, he ended the call and opened a note from the M.E.

Bernie -- I WILL be leaving here at 7pm so get your fat butt downstairs! Lots to show & ask -- Alan A.

He strode into a room shared by most detectives, found Diversi taking notes of items on his computer screen, and curtly asked: "What are you working on?"

"Karate connection. Researching how to trace what old Jim learned, and where. I've already got a lot on which dojos and Senseis trained him. Some of it is... Well, surprising."

As Cuneo pondered that, his glowering evolved to show pride in his protégé's initiative. "So, that's good. Probably. But come down to the M-E's office. Give me headlines on the way."

On the walk, Diversi said: "Jim lived in Okinawa, home of Karate in Japan, for six years. Senseis teach different styles there, but men studying Karate that long are either training to be Senseis, or rich fanatics. We know Jim's not rich, and I can't find a record of him teaching, but I read about some sort of secret study of 'ultimate killing techniques'. I haven't seen Jim's name linked to anything like it, but the records seem to be as secret as what the classes teach. This any use, Bernie?"

"Maybe. Like the Fight Club film, eh? First rule is don't talk about it. Or, it seems, record who learns it. It'd be more use if he wasn't there so long ago, but I suppose it's like riding a bike – you always know how. Anyhow, fill me in on all you found after we see Al, my M-E pal. He won't wait."

At the basement, Cuneo sent Diversi to offices and mortuary rooms to find Medical Examiner, Alan Arkey. He caught up at an examination room's door, and to the room's only live occupant, still in theater scrubs, said: "Okay, Al, I'm here by seven. Is it show or tell?"

"Q and A first," Arkey said. "May help me sort out some oddities. First, have you identified who attacked this man?"

"Not 'attacked', but I know who fought him to save a girl he was trying to mug with a Bowie knife. Why?"

"Short fight. Four injuries – three would stop him cold. I'm beyond curious... Who was the wrecking ball he took on?"

Cuneo said: "Pete... describe Mister Dawson."

Matching Cuneo's straight-faced request, Diversi said: "About five feet ten, two-thirty pounds and had bi-lateral knee replacement. And he's seventy. Did I miss anything, Bernie?"

"About covers it, Pete. Any other questions, Al?"

A frowning M.E. said: "Now I'm not sure what to ask."

"So time for the 'show' part," Cuneo said. "What have you got for me?"

As Arkey pulled back a cover from Rilke's naked body, the Detectives saw a now visible two-inch tear in the crushed throat. Cuneo studied it, scowled and said: "I hate to see even a stand-over scumbag's neck looking like that. What do your X-rays show?"

Arkey pointed to one of a lit-up array. "Need a scan for sharp details, but see where the weapon crushed the trachea just below the thorax? That killed him. Wielded right-handed, it dented the neck through the group of hyoid muscles, there. What the hell did your heroic damsel-defender use?"

"Not sure yet." Cuneo glanced at Diversi before he asked: "Do you know what broke the spine, and how?"

"Snapped at the relatively weak T-nine and T-ten vertebrae joint...also tore an external oblique muscle. That's rare. Did our hero use a hammer?" Arkey read the Detectives' faces and sighed. "Also not sure of that, eh? So you can't say if the same weapon also broke Mister Mugger's pubic bone?"

"His what?" Cuneo and Diversi chorused.

Arkey smiled and held up an X-ray. "I found that crack after seeing his bruised genitals...groin. Must've brought tears to his eyes! So... I gather you don't have all the info for my report?"

"Not quite, Al. But I do have a question... Was the fourth injury you said Rilke had in his right wrist?"

"You saw it? Yes. The radius isn't fractured, but it

took a hard blow to bruise as it has. I'll slit it open to see the extent of damage tomorrow, but I must go now. Unless you have a question?"

"Just if a theory is feasible," Cuneo replied. "I was talking to the Site Officer In Charge about it when I got your message. Picture this... Jim, our old fat man, sees a knife coming at him in Rilke's right hand, so he flings out his left hand to grab the wrist. Could that cause this degree of bruising?"

"Well, fear can fuel a hand's speed, impact and grip. So it's feasible, but I can't swear that happened."

"Good enough. So Jim has Rilke's knife hand, but is Rilke's left hand pulling Jim's right from his neck?"

"No. We'd see marks of that. His neck took a hard, fast blow with some weapon – nothing else is feasible. What do you know about the weapon... do you have it?"

Cuneo frowned. "I'll get to that. So Jim has Rilke's knife arm as their other hands flail about, trying to grip or push. His lands on Rilke's phone...say in his shirt pocket. He grabs it and he rams it up into Rilke's neck... defensively, of course. Or maybe he has it as Rilke falls on him... neck hitting the phone's edge. Well?"

Arkey mused: "Well, if you have the phone, impact would leave D-N-A to prove it. Ah. 'Not sure' again?"

"I'd say an iPhone at the scene was Rilke's. Back to our hypothesis, now with a phone weapon. As he slams Rilke's neck, unsteady old Jim falls back, pulling Rilke down on Jim's titanium knee. Or – and I can see this, Jim's defense was to knee Rilke' nuts, maybe making the bruise and break you found."

Arkey shrugged. "Seems unlikely. It explains the bruise, but not the pubic bone. Breaking it would take heavy impact."

"But possible – even if unlikely?"

"Well, yes... In court, I'd have to say it is possible."

"So what about this? Rilke recoils from the knee in

his balls – I sure would, and tries to get away. But our hero still has his right wrist, pulling him to fall back on that still raised, bent titanium knee – this time, spine first. Well?"

"You're suggesting that accidental falls on a man lying on his back with one knee up, protectively, broke both bones?"

Cuneo smiled. "Suggesting? No, only asking is it feasible? That, or maybe our fearful old man kneeing Rilke in the balls makes it just one accidental fall on his fake knee."

"Flimsy, Bernie. But a cell phone as the weapon fits the physics. A hard punch's impact is the body weight... you said two-thirty pounds, on roughly eight square-inches area of fist. Too diffused for this throat damage. A Karate chop of a hand's edge is half that area, double pounds-per-square inch impact, but still too wide to do this. A cell's edge is a square-inch, at most... eight times a fist's pounds-per-square inch impact, so possible. But can an old man use a phone to fatal effect on a fit young guy? One who... most unluckily, breaks his pubic bone and spine on the old guy's knee in one or two separate falls? Two? Two! Surely there's another hypothesis!"

"Sure. But my question was, is all I said possible?" Before Arkey could reply, Cuneo said: "Anyhow, Pete can best summarize the other hypothesis. Tell Al that theory, Pete."

As Cuneo hadn't primed him for this, Diversi began haltingly: "So... Rilke swings the knife... right-handed. Jim's left hand grabs the wrist to hold it off. But the old guy must know he can't last long against a big, fit guy who's not even half his age. So he slams a titanium knee into Rilke's...is it 'groin' I say? Rilke doubles over, and Jim throws an uppercut – but with an open hand, so it's just the fingertips that hit, and–"

"That would break the fingers!" Arkey interjected.

"I read it often does, or can dislocate them" Diversi said. "But some top Karate guys learn it as a last resort defensive blow that kills. Not so different to learning to chop through a stack of boards bare-handed, is it? So, if Jim learned to hit with his fingertips, and did it to Rilke's neck, he can let go of the knife hand, spin Rilke and fall back, pulling Rilke's spine down onto his raised knee. That about it, Bernie?"

"I'd say so, Pete. Even explains how the fight could be over in four seconds. What does Al say? Feasible?"

"Are you kidding? A seventy-year old man does all that to a big thug in four seconds? As farcical a theory as I ever heard! You can't expect me to report that's an acceptable basis for how this wrecking ball massacre could have happened, Bernie! No! The first scenario is infinitely more probable – and could even be perfect if the weapon wasn't missing."

"Oh, I agree. And so does our crime scene's O-I-C, Sergeant Niemanis. We know weapons can go missing, but I might get this one back. At worst, Niemanis will confirm it was there. Okay?" As Arkey waved-off that complication to a report of accidental death in a fight, Cuneo said: "Can I suggest that, as Niemanis believes the first scenario, you add his scene report to yours? I'll email his contact info and tell him I did."

"Fine, Bernie. But look at the time. I must run!"

"Sure, Alan. Sorry we held you up," Cuneo said affably. "Go. And thanks for calling me down."

While watching Arkey scurry back to his office, Cuneo asked Diversi: "You okay with all that, Pete?"

"I think so, Bernie – seeing Ojars and the M-E say it's the likeliest version of events. I'm glad old Jim will stay out of trouble, but... Did I hear wrong? No report includes what I found, so no one will know of Jim's years in Okinawa? Okay, it was back in his thirties, but he could've studied those secret killing techniques. The

Internet says Kyokushinkai style is brutal at any level, but are you okay with not reporting all that 'ultimate killing techniques' stuff to anyone, Bernie?"

Cuneo mimicked Diversi. "I think so, Pete – seeing it will serve the greater good. If anyone is sorry for Rilke, there'll be no info in official reports to help them sue our old guy for damages. And we not only see Jim as too nice to hassle, but I really want to believe that's true, because I want our M-E and our bosses to file, in idyllic ignorance, a version of a 'mugging gone wrong' that looks acceptably plausible."

Diversi knew Cuneo was being flippant, but he'd caught another glimpse of the inner man revealed at the crime scene. "Wait! You believe old Jim did what I told the M-E! Took the knife out of play, kneed Rilke in the balls, slammed up a finger punch into his throat, and then snapped his spine!"

"Ah, Pete ... You'll be a fine detective, after you learn what not to say out loud. Now... Want to celebrate wrapping this up with a beer or two? Somewhere quiet, so we can talk?"

KNOW THYSELF

He felt anxious about being so conspicuous at the hotel's desk to get his accreditation for this Historical Fiction Authors Association seminar. His last HFAA event was five years ago, and as he'd published nothing since, he'd be asked when the next book will come out. If truth be told, which he had no intention of doing, in that time he'd written only a few notes for a rehash of the Titanic tale, but now starring his still-undeveloped fictional characters. He'd have to rely on lies to deflect queries and, with luck, create a reputation for thorough research; if nothing else, he was now an accomplished liar.

Adam Mead woke in a sweat from that nightmare of all he dreaded, knowing other writers would see it as subconscious fear of not meeting his last book's sales. He had voiced those fears to his agent last week, and could again hear Mo Grinberg's standard attempt at an avuncular tone: "Not to worry, m'boy. Writers can't always line up words right on a page. They...you know what they...you want to get down, but sub-consciously fear that you...they haven't thought it through. That's it... Your mind has got in its head that there's a flaw in your plot that you didn't spot, and it's caused this bit of writer's block. Trust me. It'll pass. Like a kidney stone, maybe... but it will pass."

Adam had responded: "Does Simon Winchester's agent say that? No! Simon puts out nauseatingly well researched books every few years! And even Bill Bryson got out... amid all his little travel books... a History of Every-damn-thing... and a damn dictionary for writers! So why can't I be like that?"

Rather than relive Mo's agonizingly astute answer, Adam focused on the bedside clock. Seeing 3:45, he grimaced about having to endure three more hours of restless distress, but thought: *It's a... whaddayacallit? Omen... Symbol... Something. A reminder that, back when I could write, I got up at four to do it in the quiet. That dream waking me now is telling me to get back to my writing ritual. Yeah, must be.*

Adam glanced at his wife, Myra without feeling his usual umbrage for too often diverting him from writing to be sociable; he felt benevolent now the message had given him hope. He gently slid out of bed to not awaken her, and complimented himself on his thoughtfulness after succeeding.

Bypassing his study to make a pot of coffee almost dissolved his resolve; a celebratory breakfast seemed appropriate while the coffee was brewing. Making toast added delays as his search for taste-tempting toppings belatedly found the bread burning and he had to reload the toaster. As tardily, Adam came to accept his mind's malevolence in finding distractions from sitting down to write, so went off to do just that.

At his desk, he masterfully kept reading of emails and comments on Facebook posts to an hour, but then wasn't sure how to proceed. Reviewing his thin folder of notes offered no encouraging clues, and the spark of resolve that he had expected to ignite creativity seemed to be dimming. He couldn't keep a single word on his computer screen for more than ten seconds before he deleted it and, after a pause, tried another. His buoyant new self was sinking as rapidly as a gnawing sense of self-doubt was bubbling up in his mind. A glance at the clock on his computer screen told him he'd been there for another hour, so he made a bold new start; he typed a heading:

THE TITANIC: AN ADVENTURE

An hour later that was still all he had, except for a fifth mug of coffee and a looming headache that, with luck, would let him retreat to bed. But a nagging notion of needing self-discipline was being amplified by inner screams to heed the nagging, and got Adam pompously deciding: *"I must get my writing back to its best before I can be all I was."* After reflecting on that, he wistfully added: *"If I can remember what both of those were."*

"Can't sleep, honey?" Myra asked through a yawn from his study's door. "Got a flash of inspiration? I'm glad."

"Yep... fell into place." He hoped she was too sleepy to hear how hollow that sounded, but couldn't refrain from adding: "All I need to do is get its flow going."

"That's nice, hon. Love to hear about it, but I have to shower and go. We're making our pitch for Chanel's new ad campaign, and the..."

Adam heard no more; he waved, hoping it looked like considerate respect for her need, and said: "You'll hear tonight." He then gazed at the boldly titled screen, its blinking cursor a vile reminder that he might have nothing to read to her, and sought help in memories of Creative Writing classes. He remembered hearing that nothing is written until one actually writes, and advice to let first drafts flow unhindered for later shaping. It inspired him to let loose chain thoughts of thoughts for his fingers to artlessly impress on the keyboard.

~ ~ ~

It seemed just hours later, but he saw it was 7:10 PM when he heard Myra drop her briefcase, a sure sign that she was cranky, so he had to quickly evaluate what he could say he'd done. Scrolling through thirty pages on the screen had him sitting mute with shock when Myra's high-heels click-clacked into his study, bringing a curter than usual habitual greeting.

"How was your day?" Without pausing, she said:

41

"Mine was *merde*! Chanel hated our Creative ideas..."
She stopped, mouth open; she'd seen Adam scroll over
pages of text and her tone turned gleeful to say: "Your
day rocked! I'll get wine so you can read it to me in
here." It was only then that she misread Adam's dazed
expression as exhaustion. "My poor honey-bun worked
his butt off! You deserve that wine!"

Directly after his first swig of Medoc, even before
Myra was in a chair, Adam was reading aloud, one hand
held aloft to signal no interruptions. Thirty pages later,
he turned to ask: "So...?"

"So... No iceberg? The Titanic hit a spaceship from
a galaxy far, far away?"

"Umm... I think I was going for a metaphor, but it
didn't quite work. So, yes, I know I'll have to change all
that, and–"

"Don't change a word! It's breathtakingly brilliant!
More so as just a first draft. It's your finest writing ever.
And so... fucking... funny, honey!"

He hated Myra for ending the best compliment she
had ever paid him with that slur, but said only: "No one
will like 'funny' linked to the Titanic tragedy."

"Are you mad? Everyone will love how your little
spaceman just clicks his fingers to seal the hull's hole
and make the water in it vanish! And everyone will get
your satire in how the rich people on board whose lives
he's saved get him elected President. But your finale,
where he's made Planet President and clicks his fingers
to end wars and eradicate cancer, religions – all of the
world's blights... It's brilliantly funny!"

He tried to sound calm. "But not historical fiction,
which is what I write. Who I am. And it's a short story,
not a real book! Am I reduced to writing in some Sci-Fi
genre? Jesus, Myra... What about my stature as second
runner-up for historical fiction author of the year, six
years ago? That is how people know me... And like me!"

"No, Adam...absolutely no! Now you've mastered this genre – whatever it is, you can write in its style and get rich on the results, because people will love you for stories like this. It's just way too brilliant to even think about changing, and..."

Again Myra's mouth froze open, this time in horror as Adam jiggled the mouse, clicked 'Select', 'Select All', and then he tapped the 'Delete' key. She was almost too numb to hear him mutter: "A man needs standards."

FRIEND INDEED

We don't always know who real friends are until something shows us what we have, and its humbling durability. This tells of guys I didn't think of as friends until... Well, you'll see.

Jimmy Duffy's Irish imp face and grins weren't at all daunting, but those grins never warmed his ice-blue eyes. His façade-piercing gaze was as alarming as his ever-present huge friend and protector, Terry Stone. Actually, Terry had a kind nature that belied his look, but people in our distant suburb felt wary of this duo who'd been labeled Bad Boys.

I knew them from my only schooling there after my family got out of the city, sixth grade. They then went to the local High School, but my Mom said my brain needed a top-notch school, and got me into one, I think to brag about her gifted son. So I had six years of train rides for that education, and more for a Law degree, but those trains rewarded me better than academia; I met Svetlana Tovnik, who also rode them to a nerd school. Tall and elegantly pretty, she was Lana to her friends, which I ached to be. I was in awe of her poise, her pithy remarks, and mockery of my name, which my mother insisted Dad inflict on me. I was smitten, and knew it.

Teenage boys see same-age girls with mesmerizing curves as more mature than we are, so feel childish in comparison. Additionally, as I had gained weight with puberty, I doubted if a Russian goddess saw it as Mom did: cute puppy fat. Still, Lana seemed to enjoy my wit and see me as equally brainy, so one day I casually asked if she liked films. We were standing in a train, so I had to await a lull in the rattling rush for her reply.

"For clarity, Jamieson E Davison The Third... Are you asking if I'd like to see some unspecified film with you on a yet-to-be agreed night in an event somewhat akin to a date?"

I hadn't thought to define it, but said: "Well, yeah. Call it a date. This Saturday. Or next weekend. What do you say?"

"This Saturday. But to clarify again, J-E-D Three... While you are smarter than people twice your age, it doesn't qualify you for driver's licenses they can get, does it? So you won't be picking me up in a car – nor a limo. Right again?"

Lana stood so close to our shared handrail her breath tickled my lips. Amusement flared in her gray eyes, reducing me to the awkward idiot she saw most boys to be. "A... car? No, I... hadn't thought... I mean, I'd like to pick you up, but..."

"But it's more practical to meet at a Multiplex, and as you live in a farther-flung burb, it must be between us, near a train station. That should be easy, so our sole issue is the film. We don't want our first date ruined by arguing over what to see, or the choice riling one of us, so let's choose a film that neither wants to see and enjoy disparaging it over coffee afterwards. Do you approve, Jamieson E Davison The Third?"

Of course I did, but I was unable to say it because ecstasy had exploded my brain; Lana had said 'our first date'. But I'm getting way too far ahead of myself.

When I started at my exclusive High School, some old classmates resented my not joining them in the new daily jail, but not Jimmy or Terry. I later realized that those two school dropouts-to-be somehow grew to wise men who saw being judgmental as futile and got on with their lives. In my teens I just knew them to be friendly, sort of. Whenever our paths crossed, I'd begin our ritual with: "Hi, guys! How goes it?"

Jimmy would offer a mock ultra-formal salute and say something along the lines of: 'Out hiding from yer Ma coz yer not the hot shot she'd like? Be cool... Ya will be some day."

Terry's wink told me the teasing was affable before he'd add: "Yeah, stay cool. Only way to be in this life."

Time flew by, and after getting my degree I also had a marriage certificate signed by my parents and Lana's mother, whose husband had escaped to a more genial woman. We rented an apartment in the city, ostensibly for career needs, but mainly to start married life away from a scheming mother and a bitter one. As we visited our parents less often, I rarely encountered Jimmy and Terry in my old suburb, though I can't say that I went looking for them.

A memorable sighting was on a weekend that Mom had a party for her siblings and their families. Bored by my uncles' pontificating in socially myopic babble that I thought I had left at college, I decided to take Mom's pampered pooch for a walk. I don't know why I led him past the Duffy home, but I did and saw Terry washing Jimmy's Ford in the front yard. My wave was returned as a sponge's spray of soapy water in the air as I said: "Hi, Terry. How goes it? Where's Jimmy?"

While hosing a layer of foam, he said: "Inside."

"Say hi for me." I got a nod, but no grin, which was so unlike Terry that I felt vaguely uneasy, and couldn't shake it off.

Back at the party, I learned from Dad that Jimmy wasn't in the Duffys' house; he was in The Big House. Since his mid-teens he'd been in and out of jails for borrowing cars without owners knowing the borrower, so was seen as a career criminal. Police hadn't made a serious charge stick, but were content to sometimes get him off the streets, and label Terry a thug because he was Jimmy's sidekick. It didn't fit the duo I knew, but

Dad had heard it as a Justice of the Peace and Notary Public, roles that gave him local status and respect. Not from Mom; she hated Policemen coming in dirty boots to ruin her home's rugs; the ultimate crime in her eyes. Still, I had to accept that what Dad told me was true; I just wished it wasn't.

As Lana and I got busier, we visited my parents less, and if I saw Jimmy and Terry then I don't recall more than our usual banter. That changed in June last year, when my Mom and Lana's met to plan a surprise party for Lana's thirtieth birthday. In Mom's devious way, it was a trial run for a party on my thirtieth, a month later, but at the time I knew only to be there to learn what I had to do secretly for Lana's party.

One job was to have a tent put up by the pool, I assumed to isolate guests from Mom's rugs, and I opted to arrange it locally while out there. 'Old School' Mom handed me a phone book's display ad for a party gear rental shop owned by Nikos Papandria, who I'd known as a kid. As Saturday office hours weren't listed in it, I looked up his parents at the address I knew, and they gave me Nikos' cell number from. When I called, a gruff voice answered: "This is Nick."

"Jamie Davison, Nick, from way, way back. You'd be more likely to remember me as Tubby."

"Oh...yeah...brainy geek who got shipped off to a fancy High School. Real blast from the past! Wazzup?"

I explained why I'd called and voiced the hope that we could meet to lock in details while I was out from the city.

"Shit, yeah! It'll get me outta my wife's Honey Do List! Let's talk over a beer at Marty's Bar. It used to be The Grape Escape. Remember where that was?"

"I think so. I never went in there, but wasn't it near old Ma Mannix's shop full of sewing and knitting stuff? That the one? Is her shop still there?"

"It is. She isn't. Her son Mick's running it now. And yeah... Marty's Bar is right next door."

I recalled 'Mauling' Mick Mannix as the roughest Middleweight I ever saw in a boxing ring, so images of him discussing fabrics or crocheting with women made me chuckle. "No! Mauling Mickey runs his Ma's shop? That's a riot!"

"Don't let him see ya laugh as ya go by. He hates that, and he trains boxers, so he's still fit. But I'll see ya at Marty's. Twenty minutes?"

"Sure. I'm looking forward to seeing you."

It was a polite lie, but I did want to hear more about Mick. I parked where I could walk by his shop, and got as big a shock as hearing Mick ran it: Jimmy Duffy and Terry Stone were inside talking to him, about what was beyond my imagination. Jimmy's alert eyes saw me, so I waved and he nudged Terry to wave back as he offered his usual salute.

If I saw twelve motorbikes it didn't register, but the riders in gang-logoed leather were in Marty's Bar. So was Nick, as far from the grimy gang as possible, and we began our talk warily watching them get unrulier with each swig of beer. We were considering going to another bar to settle our business just as two of the gang began a fight that rolled and ricocheted along the room towards us.

"Jesus!" Nick hissed, and pointed. "The little one's a chick. That's not right!"

Before I could stop him, he dragged the man from the woman. She kicked Nick's shins. I'd have laughed, but for the rest of the gang rushing to the couple's aid. With my fighting skills limited to college boxing, and Marquis of Queensbury rules no use in a brawl that was blocking my escape to the door, I joined Nick in fending off the gang until help arrived. I was mostly hoping for it to be in the form of many large Policemen.

I have no idea how long we were fighting; seconds felt like hours as Nick and I were accumulating bruises and fast becoming exhausted. My cell phone fell from a pocket and got stomped on, so I couldn't even call for help. I could only hope that the now-vanished barkeep had called the Police, and when the gang got distracted I thought he had, but I was then able to see that Jimmy, Terry and Mick Mannix had arrived.

As Mick protected Jimmy and Terry from behind, they fought as a team, moving ahead side-by-side, As Jimmy threw a left at someone's ribs, Terry's right fist pounded the other side, and then both landed blows to the head. Gender was irrelevant to them, and I silently cheered the tactics that diverted attention from Nick and me. We helped Mick to punch anyone on the gang's flanks, and amid mounting chaos several people soon lay groaning, some wedged in bar stool legs.

It became evident that our quintet had beaten their drunken dozen, especially as Mick took weapons from all on the floor. Any alert enough to object took a blow that left them unable to see Mick fling their gun or knife over the bar. All the while, Jimmy and Terry continued tandem fighting, pitilessly beating anyone in gang gear. Their demolition of the wilting opposition encouraged Nick and me to similarly pound a nearby guy, and we began it just as a squad of Police stormed in.

I was shocked by them grabbing Jimmy and Terry along with a still standing gang member. They ignored Mick, Nick and me; apparently local businessmen and a lawyer son of a J.P. were untouchable. Any relief I felt from that, or from knowing the senior officer was in my Dad's Masonic Lodge, vanished when cops handcuffed Jimmy and Terry.

"No, not them Sergeant Kornfeld!" I yelled. "They came in with Mick to save Nick and me. Arrest the damn bike gang."

"Don't need your advice on doing my job, son. You just toddle off to yer father's place."

"No! You're missing the point! Our statements will clear Jimmy and Terry, so don't waste your time!"

The Sergeant thrust his face so close I could smell his fury. "Here's the point! Duffy an' Stone violated their Good Behavior Bonds by fighting in public, an' I can lock 'em up for that, and not let you get in the way. So don't fuck with me!"

I glanced at Jimmy, held between two cops, and he conveyed fatalistic acceptance with his consent for me to back off. The injustice to him stirred me to round on the Sergeant. "Don't you fuck with me, Kornfeld! I'll tell Dad who was to blame, and all you did and said after arriving too late to help! He'll use his position to the hilt. So forget what you want, Kornfeld. I'll see to it you can't harass Jimmy and Terry this time. So fuck off!"

Perilously purple blotches dappled the Sergeant's ruddy face while I spoke, and it was obvious that his greatest desire was to beat hell out of me. But he knew that I knew he wouldn't even threaten it, and his head slumped resignedly as he turned to tell his men: "Just the bike mob. Drag 'em back to the cells and book 'em all... And don't forget weapons charges."

Mick said calmly: "You'll find their guns, knives, and a few short lengths of motorbike chain, behind the bar."

"Thanks, Mister Mannix. You can go. I won't need a statement." To the cops holding Jimmy and Terry, he said: "What didn't ya understand about just the bike mob? Let that pair go! We'll get 'em another time... I'll be makin' a point of it."

Shaking hands with Jimmy and Terry, I told them: "I can't thank you enough. It was going downhill fast, and I hate to think how it would've ended if you hadn't come when you did. Nick and I owe you. Big time."

Jimmy's Irish grin flashed, and I even saw warmth

in his eyes as he said: "We heard the din and knew ya came in here, so friends stand by friends... doin' what ya can to help. Right? So think nothin' of it, friend."

Terry's wink told me that Jimmy's verbal shrug had covered acceptance of my thanks and the offer of theirs for preventing the Police from bashing of them. I also saw what they'd always seen: my education and life had made me as much an outsider to our old school friends as they were. Jimmy and Terry saw me as an equal. I was surprised to find I felt honored by that, and wanted to apply my new appreciation of them to others in my life with Lana. That led my thoughts to her birthday, and the surprise party at which we could reveal to our parents the new perspectives they'd have to learn in life as grandparents. We all have to live and learn.

THE BOY

Isadora despaired of ever instilling proper values in her only grandchild. She wanted to lecture him as he drove from Sunny Seniorville to her daughter Gwen's for Mothers' Day, but the boy's mind was on the road. She was sorry Gwen made her promise to not call him The Boy; it was how she saw him, even though he'd be twenty-five soon (*In July, Dora!*). She was quite willing to update the term, but to what? The Young Man? Too formal, even for her. Your Son? It was how she thought, but saying it would expose a bitter distaste for Gwen's marriage through her veneer of courtesy.

The Boy, Nicholas, reminded her of her Robert, his grandfather, who was lured into other beds enough to earn his Ex-Husband title...when? (*Twenty-five years ago, Dora... after Gwen's wedding so his adulteries weren't discussed there. We must be accurate today to put Gwen's husband in his place. We'll show him that women rule on Mothers' Day, and every day.*)

She really saw Mothers' Day as patronizing, as in: 'We men let you ladies have a day of your own'. No. We strong women deserve men's respect every day, and we don't care what men say. (*I have lived perfectly well for twenty-five years without the stupid creatures.*) As that thought surfaced, her gaze flitted over a stream of houses punctuated by shops or businesses.

"Universe Plumbing. No job too small. Are they being funny?" Hearing that aloud, not in her head, made her aware of her grandson's smirk. In an alcove of her mind, a spark of fear about looking crazy talking to herself flared as: "Yes, 'no job too small' is funny if a Universe is big. Right?"

Taking his smile as polite interest, she felt impelled to engage the boy (*Think Nicholas, Dora!*) in a worthy conversation, and latched onto the first thing she saw. "Politicians get pay rise. Did you see that news poster?"

"No, I..."

"It's outrageous! So many out of work, yet greedy politicians have the nerve to keep lining their pockets with our tax money! They're useless, anyway. Women should run the country to see things get done right. Because we would."

"Ever think of running for office, Gran?"

His question irked her, but the topic had at least evoked a response. "No. Stupid men arguing about stupid laws. I see them wasting good TV time. But if women... Look out, boy!"

As he'd begun to slow before her warning about a car racing by, she realized that he'd seen it, but it had scared her, so she had to vent. (*Show no weakness, Dora.*) "Shouldn't have a license if that's how he drives! A menace on the roads, his type. Showing off his stupid little sports car for everyone to admire. I'd ban them if I was in power!"

She sensed that his attention was fully on the car. (*911SC? What a stupid name! But remember it, Dora, to show the boy how observant we are.*) Still intent on having him reveal his views on life's values, she kept looking for items worthy of her comments while her mind sifted old memories, until... "What are you doing, Nicholas? You nearly killed us!"

"I saw the bus pulling out, Gran. No worries."

"You youngsters live in a fog! No idea what's going on! I never lost my alertness about... Why turn here?"

"Short cut, Gran."

"I never went this way. Too many corners. Main roads are best, except for stop lights. If you saw that bus, why'd you get so close? I wouldn't, and I drove for fifty-one years to last

April tenth. See? I'm still alert and know dates and things."

She saw a shrug as agreeing to her alertness, and a smile that anyone as astute as she could see as awe. She wanted him to see her mind as a genetic fountain of intellect more valuable than the superficial façade he got from Robert. She elected to do it by showing she could return to her point even after she interrupted her own train of thought. (*Keep it simple, Dora.*) "Will this short cut, with all its corners, get us to Gwen's on time? I said I'd be there by twelve, and I'm never late."

She expected him to check the dashboard clock, but he simply said: "Sure. Be there in fifteen minutes."

"I can't abide lateness. There's no excuse for it. Ever! It's just laziness, and you know I hate that. Or you should by now. Oh, look! There's a new supermarket."

She liked finding new shops to absorb free time, but knew they would bore a twenty-five year-old boy. (*If we don't think differently, Dora, he will never cease to be The Boy.*) Stifling ideas on how stores should be run, she revived the reference to laziness that had been a superbly subtle dig at Nicholas' father. More than her hunger for Gwen's lunch was a need to vilify that man for inflicting marital misery on her only child. That led her to test if Nicholas had her smart genes as well as his grandfather's handsome ones. "See that? Same poster about the politicians."

"No, didn't notice it," he replied.

She sensed impatience, which she was also feeling, as was evident in her tone. "You should've been looking for it!"

"Why? You told me about it last time."

"To show me how alert you are. I was expecting you to point it out to me, but no...I had to tell you again."

"But you'd already—"

"Nicholas! You won't be admired for being sharp at my age unless you develop it now. You should've been looking for that poster to show me how alert you are, and that you have more of my family in you than your father's. That's so important, and I'm upset by you not caring if you badly disappoint me by being just like that man."

She felt incensed by his ignoring her contempt for his father, but was glad that her real target would soon be in her sights. Better yet, she had fifteen minutes to recall the insufferable man's criticisms of her daughter to fling back at him in a destructive barrage. (*Oh, she'll say she loves him, but we'll show her he is too weak to defend himself from my clever taunts*.) She sniggered, almost inaudibly; Nicholas would see that cleverness always beats prettiness of faces.

"Lewis and Lewis Electricians. Brothers? Father and son? Two sons? Oh...that's brothers." (*You idiot, Dora!*) She saw her grandson suppressing a grin and, with all the aplomb she could manage, added: "Did you at least see that, boy?"

BECOMING BEN GUNN

Remember a Police hunt for Ben Gunn, an escapee said to be an illegal immigrant wanted for everything from shoplifting to spying? I know all about him. He's from a distant planet he calls Howff, and his real name is Navigarecon Zumonskii. It's from his job: Navigation and Reconnaissance Astronaut. Navi, as his crew knew him, was in the top rank of intelligence on Howff; here on Earth he's literally incredibly amazing.

He came here on an Intergalactic Bubblecraft while charting planets. He saw a blue one in our solar system, so flew close to see its liquid areas through a ViewPane, which he now knows to call a window. He checked his Universal Reference Tome, and would later regret not reading beyond *'the planet is no threat to civilized life'* to *'its atmospheric pressure is perilous in light craft'*. Be that as it may, as indeed it was, seeing trees that on Howff are now found only in museums induced him to fly even lower to study them; his Bubblecraft imploded.

He alone survived; he'd had time to imagine being in a tree he could see and click his fingers to actually be in it. Though sad about his crew, his own survival took priority. Sensing exhilarating atmospheric oxygen, and reasoning that one of the life forms he saw might be able to communicate, he switched on his inter-galactic translator. An implanted aural decoder told him: *"Your Nootork Stell-Cell Voca-Tome has an Earth language many of its dominant species use. Named for a minor area called England, it has use elsewhere. Why is not known, nor is if language option Urdu will be useful. Your Nootork will now automatically effect all aural and verbal translations."*

Navi finger-click moved from tree to tree, studying humans. As he looked alike enough to blend in, he did, and soon heard one say 'money makes life easier'. He pick-pocketed a twenty-dollar bill example. His voyage training in memorized molecular cloning to negate the need to haul supplies allowed Navi to covertly replicate the bill. He did it discreetly in a jacket pocket, and then as discretely slid the original back in its owner's pocket and his began life on Earth.

He paid for all his needs with memory-cloned bills, even in my bookshop, though I didn't know it at the time. He had found *Treasure Island* and, empathizing with the marooned pirate, Ben Gunn, decided to take the name. He took the book, too; walked off reading it until I yelled and he ran back to offer forty dollars and an apology. He left without his change, still reading about his new namesake and evidently glad the episode ended agreeably.

Something similar occurred in another bookshop, but its owner called Police to arrest Ben. He was taken and charged with shoplifting by Officer Liam Dolan, whose fury when Ben said that he had lifted only a book named *Catch 22* silenced Ben while he tried to decipher Police language.

"Speak up!" Dolan snarled. "Name?"

"Mine? Ben Gunn."

"That ya full name? No middle-uns?"

"Another name? Not to my knowledge."

After a taut silence, Dolan snapped: "Address?"

Ben had to ask: "Address what in particular?"

"Yer *home*, y'idiot! Wherezitat?"

"My home is, I regret, a long flight from here."

Dolan snapped: "So gimme yer I-D." As Ben had to ponder that, he roared: "Yer identifuggincation!"

"Identity? I have no document in this language."

"Got any money, then?"

"How many twenty-dollar notes do you want?"

"Whatzat? Wanna bribe me, do ya?"

"Bribe? Make an offer of an item of value to induce you to act dishonestly for my benefit? No."

Dolan roared: "Put yer money on the counter!"

"You need no counter. To produce the money I just mentally specify the number I want." As Dolan's face turned purple, Ben reached into an inner pocket of his jacket, clicked his fingers twice and then handed over two twenty-dollar bills.

"That's it? Ya got more?"

"If you wish." Ben made another forty dollars.

"Owmuch is in there? Geddit all out... *Now!*"

"My pocket is now empty, but if this is insufficient, I can produce more."

Dolan tore open Ben's jacket, ripping the pocket as he did. Ben smiled about it proving the truth, but Dolan snarled: "What's so fuggin funny? Got more in another pocket?"

"I have no others," Ben said, now so alarmed by the man's fury that he didn't enjoy having understood him. "You want more?" After four clicks in his torn pocket he pulled out eighty dollars.

That alarmed Dolan. "Howdafug'd ya do that? Got a secret pocket, or somethin?"

The Officer's stunned look induced Ben to repeat that deed. He realized his imprudence the instant that Dolan drew his pistol and snarled: "Gimme that fuggin coat to check!"

While peering into the gun's barrel, Ben clicked his fingers. Only his Howffian eyes saw it all disassemble and fall to the floor in a nanosecond of action.

Dolan whined: "Whodahell are ya to do that?"

"To clarify that, I am Navigarecon Zumonskii, but here I am to be called Ben Gunn. Please note that."

"Sure," Dolan agreed dully. "But *what* are ya?"

"A more apt query," Ben conceded. "But as you will not believe the answer, and can now over-compensate the book seller, may we not end our interaction?"

Dolan mumbled: "Wait. Lemme get it straight. Yer an illegal immigrant, givin me this two hunnerd forty bucks, right?"

"Basically, but I dispute *illegal immigrant*, so that need not concern us."

Dolan howled: "What? Arr, Jayzuz Christ!"

A senior officer came to ask: "Problem, Liam?"

"Oh, no," Dolan said; sarcastically, Ben thought. "He steals a book, tries to bribe me, then fuggsup me gun! And, Sarge... No Immigration I-D!" He looked warily at Ben to ask: "Right? Got no papers hidin in yer trick pocket?"

"No," Ben said, but added obligingly: "However, I could produce copies if shown some. Would that help?"

Sarge said tersely: "I am Sergeant Somerville, and you... are now busted, punk!"

"I doubt it. This person did use violence that tore my... fuggin coat, did you call it? But my skeletal frame still seems functionally stable."

Somerville hissed at Dolan: "I'd say it was justified violence." He told Ben: "No, consider yourself busted. Or nabbed. But arrested, whatever you call it."

"I do understand arrested." Ben informed him.

"I'm so glad," Somerville said in his own sarcastic tone before he told Dolan: "Get him in a cell...*now*!"

"Cell?" Ben queried. "A monastic institute's room, in which I can rest? I will appreciate having it."

"Stay till hell freezes over, as far as I'm concerned. Just empty your pockets first."

"My only pocket is empty, as I told this person."

"Then *this person* will take you to your rest."

As Dolan led him away, Ben asked: "Is a cell here to now be my address in this community?"

"Forever'd be good. Now geddin an shuddup!"

But Ben had to ask: "May I have my book?"

"To destroy the evidence before ya go to court?"

"I would never destroy a book," Ben assured him. "But, if not my book, do you lend reading material?"

"Nah! I'll be readin to see who else wants ya."

"No books? No matter. I shall get some later."

Dolan left, mumbling: "I get all the hard case nuts."

Ben didn't know why Dolan saw it as a hard case, as he'd admitted taking the book, but he was glad that this society provided jobs for its dimwits. It boosted his sense of gratitude for a residence, and Ben instantly fell asleep on the hard cot.

When Dolan returned, he saw Somerville waving Ben's money and saying: "Every twenty's got the same serial number!"

Dolan whooped: "Forgery! We got the bastard!"

Somerville told him: "So you make sure no other precinct's got a claim on him while I show these to the Captain."

Howffian skills allowed Ben to hear that exchange in his sleep. He woke, but heard no more as Somerville went away, so he clicked his fingers to return to my shop. Dolan, meanwhile, was finding no record of Ben Gunn in Police files and, seeing that proved Ben was an illegal immigrant, he added it to a list of charges. When forgery experts declared all the twenty-dollar bills were legal, despite their numbering, Dolan went to ask Ben about them; that began a chaotic manhunt.

Ben heard a ruckus on his return and was about to seek its cause when Somerville opened the door and stared at him, as if in disbelief. The look turned to fury as he yelled back over his shoulder: "Liam, you Celtic cretin, he's been here all along!"

"I did leave," Ben said, so Dolan's inadequacies didn't cost him his job. "But if my absence caused some concern, I apologize, and will advise you in advance of my future departures."

Men in blue uniforms and rumpled suits began to file in, and an apparently high ranking man in the latter told Ben: "Talk to me. I'm Captain Larsen. Where did you get to? And how?"

Ben held up the two books he had bought from me. "I popped out to get these at my favorite bookshop." He was proud of using an idiomatic verb. "I returned to read them in my cell. As to *how*, I traveled as I usually do when I am not flying, which I was doing when I first arrived here from home."

"Wait...what? You fly?" Larsen asked.

"Yes. I am in charge of reconnaissance missions for my government."

Larsen told the group: "There's an admission!" He asked Ben: "And which government would that be?"

"Answering that would be imprudent."

"I'd bet it could be!" Larsen said dryly, but then he spun around to address the crowd. Ben had difficulty in decoding words that seemed to tumble out as: "Tell me... Did he get Mirandad? Did he call a mouthpiece? Did we call the Feds?"

To a chorus of "no, no and no," Larsen responded: "Shit! Shit! And shit again!"

Ben was as baffled by that sounding like an order, as by Larsen's saying: "He lifts a book. We nab him. We find dud notes that test kosher. He wants to pay for the book with them. Why not? He escapes...but comes back and says he's a spy! Do we read him his rights? No. We make it easy for him to just walk away. So what are we? Fucking idiots! What are we?"

"Fucking idiots," was the chorused reply.

"You're trouble," Larsen told Ben. "I wish there was some way to make you disappear. That would solve all my problems."

"That is easily solved," Ben informed him, and with a smile he clicked his fingers.

~ ~ ~ ~ ~ ~ ~ ~ ~ ~ ~ ~

After vanishing, Ben went into a nearby hotel for a temporary home. He knew it wasn't ideal for a fugitive, so checked out next day. TV News had shown the single serial number on Ben's money, but the desk clerk didn't see it on his until Ben was outside. The clerk's howl of anger hurried Ben's finger click travel back to my shop, and that's when this seventy years old woman became fully involved in Ben's life story.

I said: "Hello again, sweetie. I didn't see you come in. Old eyes! That's not your concern. Browse away."

Ben went looking for familiar authors, though I didn't know that as I asked: "What is it you're searching for, sweetie?"

"Good writers," he replied.

"Hard to find today. Who's your favorite?"

"Kilgore Trout. He writes of life as I know it."

"Philosopher, is he? Can't say I've read him."

As Ben explained to me that Kilgore Trout was Kurt Vonnegut's authorial alter ego, two big men entered. "Customers," I said, unaware that Ben knew that they were Detectives from the local precinct. He promptly disappeared; I didn't know how then.

Returning to his Police cell was a hard choice, but it let Ben end the arduous vanishing he'd done since leaving it. He found a bulky, odoriferous man asleep on his cell's cot.

"Please explain your presence here," Ben said.

"Arrffuggovv," seemed to be the reply.

Ben shook the man, saying: "You cannot avoid me in the confines of this cell, so please awaken."

Red-lined, angry eyes opened and the man lurched to his feet, roaring: "I didn't hear ya come in my hutch!"

"You were sleeping," Ben reminded him. "Sergeant Somerville gave me this 'hutch', and Captain Larsen did not object to my having it, though at some later point he did express a desire for my absence."

"Whaddaya blabberin about?" The hulk growled, confusion now matching his hangover-fueled rage.

"I am telling you that this is my cell. If, as it seems, you wish to voice a contrary opinion, please know that I would appreciate civility. And that should begin with introductions. I am Ben Gunn."

"An I'm rippin yer head off!" He lunged at Ben, but found himself choking the cell door until he saw Ben near the cot and sprang over there, only to then see Ben was back at the door. Now stunned, he mumbled: "Fast little bastard, ain't ya?"

"That is astutely observed...I can be a fast bastard," Ben said, glad of a vulgarism to aid communications. "So please stop trying to hurt me and let us talk."

The man lunged, and again hit the door, but saw Ben in the adjacent cell and began wailing of a need to "geddorf dabooze". Ben returned to the pitiable hulk, who closed his eyes to chant: "If I can't see ya, ya can't be here, if I can't see ya, ya can't be..."

"I can fully satisfy both our needs," Ben interjected gently. "If you sleep in that cell and I reclaim my own."

A red eye peeked at Ben as the big man mused: "If ya ain't here, I shouldn't hear ya... an what I hear's no help. I can't go there, coz I'm locked in here. But yer not in here... so ya can go in there, an not be there, too."

"That theory actually confuses me," Ben admitted. "But it seems to entail relinquishing my cell, which I reject. As for being locked in here, I assure you that need not be. But first, back to introductions. What is your name?"

"Bert...Albert," the quavering voice replied.

"Well, Bertalbert, may I effect my suggestion?"

Taking his silence as assent, Ben held Bert's arm, clicked his fingers and both rematerialized in the next cell. Another click left Bert alone, whining promises to some deity that he would "never touch annuver drop".

I have learned that enduring quark realignment for disappearing and rematerializing is debilitating when done frequently; Ben needed to rest. But with Bert's loud and constant groans thwarting that, he chose to risk overloading his quark network by leaving there to revisit my shop.

Apparently it was as his finger click took him to me that Sergeant Somerville stormed in, yelling: "Shut up Bert or I'll..." A minute passed before he could add: "How the hell did you get in *there*?"

Bert wailed: "Sarge! Aw, geez, am I glad ta see ya! I think I'm in the horrors real bad! Real, real bad!"

"*You* are?" Somerville queried. "Seeing you in *that* cell has me thinking *I'm* the one with the D-Ts!"

Bert raved of a fast little bastard darting about his cell, but not really in it, so Somerville asked: "Did he look like a guy in the other cell who's not there now?" As Bert shrugged and could offer only the name Ben Gunn, Somerville said: "Jesus, Bertie, I was hoping you wouldn't say that."

"Ya do believe me, Sarge? I ain't makin it up... I don't think."

Somerville said he believed every incredible word and told Bert to block it all out with sleep. Bert fell back on the cot, but his eyes stayed wide open as he asked: "But whaddif I see him wiv me eyes shut, Sarge?"

"Open them. If you can still see him, call me."

"Orright, but come quick. He's a bad fast bastard."

"Seems so," the Sergeant muttered as he left.

Ben would later see TV news reports about Police investigating his disappearance and the hunt for him being extended to members of The Magicians' Guild.

By then, though, he had a sanctuary.

On arriving at my shop, he heard groans and found me in agony at the foot of stairs to my apartment. I said feebly: "Fell. Coming from... bathroom I... Please... call for an ambulance."

I now know why he didn't; he'd seen Police arrive with ambulances on TV shows, and if that happened his quark core was too frail for him to vanish again. Ben would have healed me, but as it would reveal he wasn't human, he feared that I would fear him.

"Please phone. I think I've broken something."

He suppressed his concerns to say: "I can better heal you than medical practitioners here, but you must trust me, and I you. What I do must stay secret."

"Do it, sweetie," I said, but then I passed out from the pain and the strain of trying to speak.

Ben was too anguished to realize that I had again asked for an ambulance, but he saw my plight. He ran a hand over me, identifying breaks in my ribs, hands and legs, and he was examining cuts and bruises on my left arm as I stirred. He smiled reassuringly and, he later told me, opted to ease me into all I was about to witness by starting on minor wounds.

He took a hanky from where I tuck them under my sleeve. I couldn't believe that he'd waste time on magic tricks, but after he put the hanky on my arm and clicked his fingers, he took it off to reveal my skin was healed. I watched in awe as he cured each cut and bruise that way, and I had to say: "It's a miracle! But it's a shame you can't fix whatever's broken as easily."

"Same method, just much slower," he told me. "But I regret having to recoup my energy before I can do that for you. More so, I regret that the delay will prolongs your pain."

I forced a smile to say: "Ambulance could've been here by now. Not too late to call... Is it sweetie?"

That provoked Ben to go on; he gently touched a broken rib, clicked his fingers, and then held the stairs' banister. Each time he did it I saw his energy ebbing while I felt my relief growing, so I said: "More miracles! I can breathe again!"

"Yes, but please remain still. I repaired broken ribs so they do not pierce a lung, but I must rest before I use more energy on other bones. I am sorry for the delay."

"You fixed *broken* ribs?" I queried incredulously. "How?"

"Given that your bone damage and my exhaustion are negating activity, I have time to explain that. But I must ask you to never tell anyone what you learn, and I must trust you to know this. Do you agree?"

"Of course. Who'd believe this fix for broken ribs?"

"Thank you. But before I reveal my unearthly skill, I must know to whom I am doing it. I call myself Ben Gunn. You are?"

"Ellen Brettelle. Ellie, to friends."

Ben told me of his having been the Navigation and Reconnaissance Officer of a spaceship, and of escaping to a tree as it crashed. When he talked of now being too far from Howff to be rescued, my tears welled up, and he thought my pain was bad with him too weak to keep healing me, so I said: "I'm just sad, sweetie. If all you say is true...and I do believe it after all I saw... you are lost to your family. Are you married?"

"On Howff, we bond with whom we feel content. In my reading about Earth marriages, contentment is not given priority. But... No, I am not bonded."

I smiled, perhaps ruefully. "We value contentment too late in life. If we looked for it as young adults, we might find successful marriages."

Ben agreed it was likely, and furthered our evolving rapport by continued his story. He was relieved when admitting he was the object of the Police hunt in TV news didn't bother me. What stirred up my emotions was his obvious concern about being unable to find lodgings where he would be safe from persecution.

Perhaps triggered by an instinctive reaction, I was inspired to say: "Live with me! I get so few visitors that it will be safe. And a way to repay you." I blushed. "But I should admit to being selfish. I'll not only get to enjoy your company, but also have you to fix me if I fall."

He smiled dismissively, but warmly. "I thank you for offering not only a home, but also opportunities to assist you. You are so generous that I believe living with you will make me content."

He returned to repairing my broken bones with his finger clicks while explaining the technique. "Faults in quarks and molecular structures cannot vanish, so I get them by absorbing your damaged molecules into my body for dispersal in inanimate objects."

"Sorry, but... Where did my broken bones go?"

"Not bones, only mutated molecules of breaks in them. I transferred those molecules to the stairs' rail. Wood is dense, so it does not feel pain, and is not even weakened by the process."

"So... You had my broken ribs in you before you put... their molecules in the wood? All my pain too?"

"Yes. That is the process. And it is why I must rest, regrettably prolonging this. But I am glad you have no tumors. Removing them is harder."

"What? You can get rid of cancer? How?"

"Similarly, with greater concentration that is even more tiring. Teams do it on Howff. But now, as your repairs are done, may I accept your offered home? My need to rest is becoming irresistible."

I nodded and stood up. Ben had said that I would be pain-free, but I felt livelier than I had in years as I helped him to his feet. Smiling about that, I helped him upstairs to my apartment, with its old lady decor. He has since told me he sensed calm harmony in it as we went through to my room, where he sprawled on the bed, instantly asleep.

I sat by him, reviewing all I'd learned and reliving his gentle healing touch. I remember thinking it, but must have mused aloud: "Such a sweet man! I wish I were young again. I would give him contentment... I'd content his brains out!"

"I shall regress your age after I feel fully rested," Ben said softly from his sleep.

Originally published in 2015 by The New Atlantean Library
In the anthology "7 VOICES" by North Fork Writers Group

Finding Out

Yes, it's exactly how I remember the view. The land falls sharply from the edge of the road to a long, gentle slope that ends at those rows of elm trees. Yeah, and beyond them is something unknown that has haunted me all my life. Wow. Amazing to see it all again after so long, but it's good to see no developer ruined this area of natural beauty so close to the city. It's a far cry from where my grandparents' home stood behind where I am now. The block of land it used to be on now has one corner of the first of a row of ugly high-rise mini-cities of condos.

Still... The hill and trees remain quite a sight, but of course everything looks bigger than when I saw it as a kid. Those elms especially. Yes, seeing them has it all coming back. I can still hear Grandma telling me – and bossily, I thought, even then – not to go through those elms. In fact, she said I shouldn't even go near them, and I remember her saying: "Promise you won't, Tony. There's something beyond those trees that you never want to see. Just believe me... Don't go there... ever. So promise me, Tony."

I started promising that from when I was nine, the year Dad disappeared. He'd left home on the morning after my ninth birthday to come up and help Grandpa paint the house, but Grandpa said he never got here. He was just gone, he'd left us, and that's when Mom moved us to this outer suburb, as it was then, to live with her parents. I remember Mom was always crying during our year here, and she stayed miserably sad for six years after, until she gassed herself on car exhaust in the garage of the home we'd rented.

71

I cried about Dad in that first year, too, but I was diverted from that a bit by being a new kid trying to fit in at the school here, so my grandparents told people that I wasn't affected by losing him. It wasn't true, and anyway, a month later my tears were for my dog. When I got home from school one day, Grandpa told me Tico had run away. I said he'd never leave me, and Grandpa said that maybe he went off looking for me. That made me cry. Grandpa never liked us bringing my dog here, and I don't think he was at all sad about us losing him. But the sorrow that stuck with me was in knowing that loyal Tico didn't find me. I knew he'd keep on searching and be gone forever, just like Dad.

Still, I promised Grandma I wouldn't go near the elms, so I didn't while I lived with her. But thirty-odd years later, I'm here without her or Mom to tell me to stay away from those damn trees, and no good reason that I can think of to keep sitting in the car looking at that forbidden area. I could go and investigate what the fuss and fear was about, but do I really want to drive around to that twisting bumpy track to go down to it? Or get out in this mist and fight through what looks like thick scrub that's grown in the gully between where the slope ends and the first of the long rows of elms?

Sure. Why not? Finding out at last is something to do, and why let some damp air and bushes stop me?

~ ~ ~

Now I know why I should have done that years ago, but I wish I hadn't done it today. The mist turning into a constant light rain and the scrub turning out to be thorny briar bushes were easier to deal with than what lies beyond those elms. It's a small cemetery that must have belonged to old church that's now a ruin, and it looks like no one has been in the cemetery for years. But in all the long grass I found a little headstone that has Dad's name on it. I know it's not someone with the same name, because it has his birthday and the date he died, the day after my birthday. That's when he went to help paint my grandpa's house – and the last day I ever saw him.

I know what that means. For thirty-odd years I've gone through life not knowing that my Dad didn't walk out on Mom and me, as my grandparents kept telling us. Their doing that was more evil than wicked, but it's even worse to find that my grandfather was a lying shit, and not know if he got Grandma to lie, or if he'd lied to her. It will take time to figure this out, but I'm already angry about not knowing what that despicable old man might have done to Tico. Now there's no one left alive who knows, or who could even help me to find out.

HEART ACHES

There's coincidences, amazing coincidences, then this - too magical for words... That's what Darren Scott thought he told Julie at their chance encounter earlier today. It was inaccurate, but he liked to star suavely in memories. What he accurately recalled of their meeting in a Deli was her initial iciness after thirty-plus years. But now, seeing her twice in the one day, he had to focus on Julie, who was heading off in the distance and unaware of him chasing her. This time he recognized her hair-matching, silver-gray coat as he walked out of the hospital, peering down the road to where he parked before the numbing time by his father's bed. An image of Julie in that coat had filled his mind since the Deli and subsequent move to Starbucks; it was all he'd had to boost his mood in the dismal hospital.

Between them a train station was disgorging a mob into his path, but his mind was on recalling all about her so he could be sweetly wistful when he caught up. Going into dispersing commuters, he felt the stress of rushing, but was resolved to not lose Julie after their long Starbucks tête-à-tête left so much unsaid, unasked and, crucially, unanswered. He endured the protests of his lungs and legs by remembering their first kiss, but had to ignore the image of her having to lower her lips to his as she had said: "So big girls are out of your reach, huh? Don't worry...this one will come down to you."

Like salmon heading upstream into rapids, Darren pushed against the crowd, his mind flooded by images of Julie at Starbucks as he struggled to keep her in view. He knew he mustn't let her slip out of his life again, and that thought began him pondering the unlikely events that led him to here today. Why choose to not take the Freeway? He had time to kill before hospital visiting hour, but slow traffic frayed his usually cool style. And why stop to buy a cigar? His Cardiologist banned them now a stent nested in an artery, and he rarely missed cigars, but an inexplicable desire for one had surfaced today and he'd stopped his car then and there.

~ ~ ~

Choosing that seedy area's Deli after he saw teens doing drugs outside was a miracle. They had a bag of 'fruit salads', stolen multi-colored meds with a variety of long-lasting effects, often for a suddenly shortened life. Disturbed by that as he went in, Darren had been glad to see that he could get out quickly. Of two swarthy shopkeepers, one was serving the only customer, a tall woman in a silvery-gray coat that looked too classy for the district. As the second man greeted him, that coat and the woman's profile drew Darren's eyes again.

"Jules?" He could hear his incredulity. "Is it Julie Pierce?"

"It hasn't been Pierce for... forever." She'd looked down saying that, as if nervous, but turned toward him and calmly added: "Hello, Darren. I wondered if you'd speak to me."

"You recognized me? Why not say something?"

Her reply was soft and hesitant. "Oh... You know."

"All I know is that some coincidences are amazing, but this one's magic. Why not say hello after so long?"

"Well, we didn't part so magically, did we?" With that gentle rebuke, her hazel eyes twinkled mischief.

As crinkles radiated around eyes that once excited him, Darren was unaware that her pretty face showing few signs of her age. His mind was scrambling to reach back beyond decades, but he saw a wry smile twitch her lips and managed to mumble: "We didn't?"

"No, but let's not reminiscence now. Buy what you

want, and then I'll let you buy me a coffee somewhere."

"Great! It'll just take a sec."

He saw Monticristos amid cheap cigars and raised one finger to the shopkeeper as he pointed. He spun back to Julie in time to see her slip a pack of cigarettes in her bag, and felt relief from having a safe topic to restart a conversation. "Both needing a smoke is fate! And shows that smoking can't be all that bad for us." A memory flared, and he added: "Still menthols?"

"Lights. Token health gesture. My only vice now."

Paying for the cigar diverted Darren's mind from cute retorts, but one escaped. "Whatever you're doing for your health, Jules, it works. You look stunning!"

He thought she'd ignored the compliment, but as they walked to the door, Julie said quietly: "You haven't changed."

"Yeah, right. My hair's going white, and I didn't lug this weight around with me back then."

A glow he felt faded as she gave him a head to toe glance, smirking. "I didn't mean how you look."

After leading the way to his Audi, Julie pointed to a shiny old Mercedes 450SE and told Darren to tail it to a Starbucks. He was about to praise how she cared for her car, but realized that she must have known his car by seeing him get out of it. Again wondering why she'd ignored his arrival at the Deli, Darren hoped to remember why they'd split before he got to Starbucks. He drove, picturing their year-long affair when he was singing in a band. Julie hadn't seemed jealous of the groupies, nor of his fiancée, Laura, so he had chosen to believe that she was content in their secretive affair. The fallacy in that itched in his mind back then, but not enough to scratch at the surface.

A Barber Shop beside Starbucks reminded Darren that a trim before going to the hospital would end his wife's nagging, and he was sure that Julie's prickliness would curb chatting to give him time. Seeing a woman cutter buffet her customer with hefty breasts decided the matter. He was grinning as he opened Starbuck's door for Julie, whose quizzical expression he ignored.

She sat at a small table and asked Darren to get her whatever Starbucks call a cappuccino, a request that was sweetened by flashing eyes that had him feeling almost young again. It led to him ignore another of his Cardiologist's mantras; he returned with a cappuccino and a double espresso.

"I see your love of drinking mud hasn't changed."

Rather than risk revealing his heart attack, he said only: "But less now. No, I want this to be like old times, when we'd sit chatting in coffee shops for hours on end. They were the days!"

"Nights," Julie said, quite tersely. "After I'd waited for the gear to be packed... if I was lucky enough to be allowed at your band's gig. Remember that?"

Darren's affable façade wilted, but a hint of sparkle in her eyes kept him willing to stay, mostly to say: "Ah, whatever I did back then to bury a burr in you, Jules, I'm really, really sorry. But I've racked my brain and... See, my memories of us are great. Apparently not all of yours are. So... What was it?"

She tried to laugh, but his intense gaze eroded her act. "Great? Really? No, it's too long ago to fuss about. Let's talk of now. What're you up to? Last I heard, you were in advertising."

"Got out. Too many 'poseurs', as we used to say. We were so pretentious! But, no... I don't want to change the subject, Jules. Won't you answer my question?"

Julie stalled by pulling the new cigarettes from her bag, glancing at a NO SMOKING sign and returning them. "Back then, I would have done anything for you, Darren... Too often I did. It still hurts that you never knew how much I loved you."

"But we were kids having fun, not... you know."

"You were the kid! Having fun with every girl you could. But I clung to any time you gave me, hoping you would see I wanted you all to myself. My big hope... stupid as it was... was for you to love me like I loved you. So what did you do? Not change... Married Laura and, I heard, ruined her life by still having love affairs. No, not love. Flings! Heart-breaking flings!"

The response in Darren's mind seemed sure to drop him in the pit her tone had dug under his façade, but he let it out. "Thirty years ago! You talk like it was yesterday. I was no saint, but why be so tough on me? Can't we just be glad to have met up again? Maybe I did deserve that lecture once, but I... No, sorry... I'm trying to say that I don't get this hurt you've hung onto. Not having me in your life didn't stop you getting on with it. You look great. Nice clothes... classic car... all good. Want to take a shot at explaining it? Please?"

She lowered her gaze to her hand, as if willing it to stay steady while lifting the cup to her lips. He kept silent, and used the seemingly long pause to admire her retained beauty, seeing a ghost of flowing honey-brown waves in her gray hair. He also saw a missing wedding ring's groove in her finger; it helped his expression to turn to compassion as Julie spoke, sounding more like she was explaining to herself, than to him.

"Sorry. Emotions are... shaky. I lost my husband. Four months ago. Cancer. It's evil. For years I watched him fade, suffering as it spread... losing the will to fight. The end was a blessing, but it left me... You know. So I'm sorry... I just ..."

He held her left hand, unconsciously feeling the groove as he said: "No need to say more. Or apologize. I'm sorrier than I can say, Jules. I saw two uncles... fade like that. No one should go through it. Not the dying, or who's left behind."

79

"No," she said firmly. "I must... explain. When life is bad, you think of what might have been. I couldn't... without thinking of you... a lot. So seeing you get out of your car was a shock... my memories were right there. I had been thinking that if I'd done things differently I might have won you from Laura." Julie tried to smile. "It's funny. Over the years I've often imagined us as a couple... having coffee together, just like this."

Darren's stifled chuckle cleared Julie's mind to register that his index finger was tracing the ridge on her ring finger. She slid her hand from under his to lift her cup with both, then gazed into his eyes, unwilling to say more.

He hoped his expression looked reassuring. "Sorry. I guess what you said drew me to where your ring had been. I was surprised you don't wear it. Forget that. It's irrelevant. I was trying to muster up small talk."

"John wanted it with him. I didn't mind. It's ash now. No. Gold melts, right? Anyhow, it's gone. And it'd be silly to wear just an engagement ring at my age. But this isn't worth talking about. Tell me about your life. Not serious like I just... Make me laugh. You always could. That was one of the things I most... Oh, I don't know. Tell me anything."

"In my second marriage." His pause for a laugh was rewarded by a smirk. "Yeah. Big surprise. Ten years. Laura and I stayed friends, but she's better off without me. Marriages get to be a pattern, don't they? And if the pattern has a flaw, like unfaithfulness, it repeats. I did try to be a good husband. Really. But I was always ready to bed hop. Lousy thing to admit, but you know it was true. Why hide it?"

"Do you treat this wife better? Tell me about her."

"Cheryl's a good kid. And we're good for each other. Being different as chalk and cheese complements all we lack individually. She's practical, too...do anything she puts her mind to. Me? Well, you said it. Still a kid in my head, chasing dreams. But I've learned to shrug about what I can't do. This body keeps reminding me I'm not a kid any more."

Julie seemed to deliberately avoid the topic of age as she asked, too gaily: "What dream are you chasing?"

"Now? Writing...a novel. Still more like just a heap of stories."

"About?"

"Life, I suppose."

"Yours? Now there's a colorful tale!" She softened that sarcasm with a smile.

"Not exactly mine. But I borrow bits from it."

"Do I rate a mention?"

Darren sipped his espresso to stall; one story had a tall band groupie whose soulful moans during sex led the singer to write sad love songs. After lowering his cup, he said flatly: "It's fair to say I blend aspects of people I know, or have known, to make my characters. I guess that's what fiction is... It works for me."

If that disappointed Julie, it showed in her change of subjects. "You called your new wife a kid. A young trophy? There's a surprise." She arched an eyebrow.

Darren chuckled to hide the relief of not having embarrassed her. "Hell no! Almost my age. As for your other question... I've given up frolicking with strange ladies... and some were real strange! So age does have benefits, like putting an end to all that bed-hopping. Oh, sure, I still look. Just not up close."

"So laudable." Julie's lips had a wry smile. "Cheryl is a lucky lady... First woman to have you all to herself."

He chuckled. "Yeah. Real lucky. What a prize."

A shadow of seriousness darkened Julie's eyes, but a bright smile cleared it. "And that hasn't changed... I'm glad. You're the most open man I ever knew. Say what you think, with none of the games men play. It won't be news to you...given all your experience, but we women love honesty almost as much as a man's ability to make us laugh."

"Write that down. I'll show it to Cheryl next time she's giving me hell for it."

"Giving you hell for what?"

"Not engaging the brain before driving my mouth. Like, if we're at a friend's home and he asks how I like some new thing he bought... I tell him the truth. That's sparked a few ear-bashings in the car ride home."

In Julie's laugh he heard an echo of her naked at a park with him, stoned on pot and Chablis, and giggling at a family hurrying away from the sight of them. He added a chuckle as he asked: "Know what just came to mind?" As her curiosity showed, he declared: "A loaf of bread, a jug of wine, and thou beside me. Pretty soon I'll be fat, drunk and in trouble for spooking good Christian picnickers. Remember?"

Her laugh bubbled again as she said: "In the park... that Sunday you gave up band practice to be with me! Oh, yes! I often think of that." She paused, apparently checking if what she said crossed a privately defined line, but then shrugged. "Well, as I told you. I've done a lot of thinking lately."

While no other Starbucks' customers that day saw a wall fall between the older couple there, Darren and Julie did as they revived the past with: "Do you ever see...?" The reply was always 'no'; both had left their suburb soon after the affair and each new home took them farther from people they'd known. Neither let any pain from old times mar a rekindling of the glowing bond they'd had, nor said more than needed if they had to refer to their marriages. They squeezed each other's hand to convey delight at anecdotes, and by the time Julie saw that an hour had vaporized, they were simply holding hands.

"Hell! I'll be late for my appointment!"

Darren then saw a blur of movement. Julie's hair swirled in unison with her coat's hem as she swooped up her bag and strode to the door. He had to keep up; the most important fact had not been revealed.

"Jules! Don't go until I get your phone number!"

"No time! I'm late... Give me your business card."

Before they reached her car, Julie had a cigarette alight while Darren was still finding a card in his wallet. She opened her door, then spun back to get his card, but he held it tightly.

"It's old, but the home number's right. You will ring?"

"Yes." Her eyes pleaded to excuse her haste, but then flashed with mockery. "And if Cheryl answers?"

"Ask for me. I'll say I ran into you today. Probably."

"You would." She leaned in to kiss his cheek, but he held her arm to extend the contact. "Darren! I must..."

"Yeah, an appointment. Too important to stay?"

Julie's exhaled smoke as she again showed regret. "It's... grief counseling... More... helping get my head straight. She's a shrink, and a friend of friends who knew John. It's why I'm in this area, and why I can't be late. I'd look like I'm not interested. She does help... and I've talked about you, so after seeing you... I think I need to talk to her. I know I do."

Another swirl of the coat had Julie in the car and the engine of the 450SE rumbling to life. Then she looked up at Darren and smiled. "I am glad we... met up. And I will call."

As soon as the door clicked shut, she spun the steering wheel and the Mercedes sped into the patchy traffic. Darren could only wave, and hope she saw that in her car's mirrors.

~ ~ ~

Now, with that vivid in his mind, he emerged from the crowd of train commuters and saw Julie's Mercedes again, parked a few cars from where she was walking. As she was close enough to drive off before he got to her, Darren wanted to run, but closing the gap to her had turned breaths to gasps. He saw it as just a heart attack's aftermath, so no cause for alarm, but felt it wise to suck in a big breath and yell: "Jules! Wait!"

He saw her pause briefly and glance back before going on to her car, where she stopped and peered back at the dispersing mob. That reminded him that she'd always had weak distance vision. With flailing arms that would look odd in any other setting than people pointing to where cars were parked, he caught her eye. His relief from that was fleeting; an obviously agitated Julie checked her watch.

She waited, fidgeting with evident impatience until he had almost reached her, then called: "I've got to go, Darren! I said I'd phone!"

"Yeah, yeah. But —"

"No buts! I..." By then, he was close enough for her to see him gasping; her tone changed. "Good god! Are you having a heart attack? Quick... I mean gently... sit in the car! Get your breath. Are you okay? No, don't speak! Do I call for an ambulance? Oh, my God!"

Darren eased backwards into the front passenger door that she held open and sat with his feet still out of the car, then forced a wan smile. Amid gulped breaths, he quipped: "Don't call me God, Jules. But thanks. Actually...had a heart attack. Few months back. But I'm fine. Or I will be. Really."

"Can I get you some water? There's a shop just over the road." Her caring concern put a tremble in each word, and as her face lost its mask of impatience, her tears welled up.

"I'll be fine, Jules. Can I just sit here a minute? Can

you spare the time?"

"Of course! Then I'll drive you to your car. Where did you park? Why are you here?" Regret at peppering him with questions showed in quivering lips as she added: "I mean... That's if you feel up to driving. Should I take you home?"

"My place, or yours?"

"Darren!"

"A joke, Jules. I'll be good to go in a minute...but a lift to my car would be sweet...if you can spare –"

"Forget it! Forget I was... I'm sorry I was bitchy. Nothing matters now, except to be sure you're all right. So wait while I get you some water. No arguments!"

Darren turned to watch her glide across the road to a Deli, and smiled at this meeting also involving one as he swung his feet in and closed his eyes. Above the traffic's roar he could hear his pulse's soggy thumping. His anxiety about that faded as the sound did, and by the time Julie returned and sat beside him he was feeling almost at ease.

"Here. Sip some water." She handed him a large bottle of Deer Park. "Not too much. Take it easy."

Darren grinned. "What a brand image-problem! Our water's either from a park full of deer, or a spring in Poland."

"Good! Back to your old self. Your color's better, too. You looked... Well, I was really worried about you."

"Must admit...so was I. I feel okay now, but can I sit a few minutes? I'm sorry if I'm holding you up."

"Forget it. There's no reason for me to race off."

"But from how you were as I got here, I thought—"

"I didn't know how to talk to you after being... But the reality is..." She shook her head, as if to dislodge a thought, but a nibble of her lip exposed her failure.

"There's some great truth you can't tell me? Why?"

Julie frowned. "I...can't say." She got her cigarettes

and was about to light one. "No! I can't fill you up with second hand smoke if you had a heart attack. Sorry."

"Jesus, Jules! I didn't buy my cigar as a souvenir of that place I met you, so... Go on. Light up."

"Really?" Taking a chuckle as consent, she lowered her window. "Thanks. I tried to stop, but... they helped me cope with John's... Better to stop and just drink, but to wine and cigs I added vodka. I'm back to only wine."

"My Cardiologist says that's okay. Banned every damn booze you can think of, but said a little red wine's good for us. He didn't define 'a little'... I didn't ask."

Julie's smile was the first since he arrived. "Still my old Darren... Hopeless! Never did let doctors tell you how to live."

"Think they're gods! Your smile makes me feel better than any doc could. And so does still being your Darren... even labelled old."

Her smile vanished, replaced by an expression he couldn't read, but sensed it told of inner conflict. Being unable to ask what it was, he took a sip of water. She finally spoke, without looking at him, and he became more baffled by her rambling musing's bitter edge.

"Why would a shrink lecture me? I thought they help you see things for yourself... but... See, I tried to brush you off because that didn't happen. I know I started it... being late. It got Riva... the psychiatrist, cranky. But I said I ran into you and she asked how I felt about it... I let it all out. She always says to say what I'm thinking. But, hell! I did, and she really let loose on me. I was... still stunned by it when I saw you."

Rather than risk an impromptu response that she might find inappropriate, Darren filled the silence by watching Julie gnaw her lower lip and gaze blindly at traffic. Evidently sensing his scrutiny, she spun toward him, but didn't speak. He offered a smile that he hoped looked sympathetic, but it faded as she focused on his face. Hers took on a look of surprise, as if only now seeing him, and she diverted to what he assumed was safer terrain for her.

"You've had a haircut. It looks... nice."

"It's too short. I should've known better than to get it cut in that lousy area where we had coffee. Serves me right."

"By that Starbucks, I bet. Miss big boobs cut it?" She then assessed the nuances of Darren attempt at a blasé nod.

The short silence felt alarmingly long, so he tried to laugh it off with: "Yeah.,, she'll be a big girl when she grows up, eh?"

"So the haircut's why you're still up in this area?" Her question clearly included reference to the buxom haircutter.

Darren said only: "It just filled time before going to the hospital, back the other side of the station."

Alarm tore through Julie's pensiveness. "A heart check-up? After a double espresso got to your blood pressure? That's so...! God, Darren! If I'd known, I wouldn't have let you drink it."

"I said don't call me God." He hoped his smile didn't show his delight in her care about his health. "No, I visited Dad. Not that he knows... had so many strokes he's always out of it. But I've got to go. You know how it is."

"I do... It's... hard. I'm so sorry, Darren." After a pause, she said: "And I know you two fought back then, so it's good of you to go now... but tough, I bet. Does your mother visit? Or isn't she still... She'd be very old by now."

"A feisty eighty-two... hasn't seen Dad in twenty years. Still hates him. As their only kid, I'm stuck with that. Your shrink can tell you about symbiotic bonds... couples thrive on hostility. I know more... raised in the shadow of one." Darren then thought to say: "How are your folks? I really liked them."

"Both gone... last year, when John's cancer was raging."

Julie tossed her cigarette butt out the window, and when she turned back, Darren saw her tears and took her hand. He then raised his other hand and gently lowered her head onto his shoulder, saying: "Sorry. Didn't think before I spoke. At our age... likely they, or one of them, had... But I... Sorry, Jules."

"I'm... just shaky. They both passed quickly... not too bad. But odd. Dad was really healthy, but when she went... heart attack, he just... died. A month later."

"It's sort of nice." His tone told of awe. "Not you losing them, but... the fact he couldn't live without her. Love like that is nice."

Julie raised her head to look into Darren's eyes. "As lovely as life gets... happy together. My sister Wendy and I were lucky to grow up in that love. I've thought about that a lot over the years. Especially lately."

Reminded that she'd admitted to thinking about him, Darren realized that their day's conversations had come full circle. It seemed wise to end them there, before anything too unnerving was said, but he couldn't break their locked gaze. It took all his willpower to say: "Time's getting away. I should, too. Still want to play chauffeur, and take me to my car?"

"Yes." The bland reply was at odds with the intensity of her eyes as they peered into his. "If you think you're ready and want to go now."

"Honestly? Going's now must be about the last thing I want...but, really... I should."

A frown flittered over her brow before she said softly: "Should I worry about you driving? Should I follow till you get home? You know...to be sure you're okay."

"No. Thanks. I don't think so."

Julie expelled a long sigh, which Darren interpreted as regret for having to end this unexpectedly warm reunion. He read her lapse into pensive silence the same...until she spoke.

"Then would you like to follow me home to my place?"

New Bloom

She froze briefly, that pulse between resignation and taking the next step to who-knew-what. She knew. She would be naked. Worse, he would see her with eyes attuned to how his generation looks at life.

If only he'd seen me at his age...or even... Damn!

He'd see breasts that still grabbed attention in low-cut tops, but hung near her waist without a bra, and she wondered if his generation saw only firm and perky as beautiful. Before the breasts, the matronly bra with its sensibly wide straps to hoist Double-D loads, and long sides to hold in what she used to be able to laugh-off as love handles.

If only I'd thought to wear a lace one... If only I'd thought!

She could slide the cotton panties down with her skirt, but how could she hide the shameful bra? Could she keep the blouse on until she'd dropped the skirt and panties? Wouldn't that be too provocative? Too blatant? She did it anyway.

Maybe undressing at his age is an unexciting prelude.

She watched him peel off his shirt, muscles alive with action, and knew that she had never seen such masculine beauty. She had no way to retreat now, no painless way to hide the woman she'd become. With a deep breath, she slid the blouse from her shoulders and sleeves from her arms.

How stupid... standing here in just a bra! Oh, please know that if I'd really believed that tonight we might... Please!

She prayed her panic didn't show and hoped to be

able to gauge what he was thinking, but knew only that she must try to be brave and face him, She resolutely turned to do that.

Oh, too blatant! Will it make him feel trapped if...
"Want another glass of wine?"

That's what he's thinking about? Now? Why?

If he could see that she needed a drink, was she so obviously embarrassed about standing there, exposed, waiting for one of them to make a move to the bed?

Does he need one? Is he stalling? Oh, well...

"If you're having one... Sure. Why not?"

Did that come out sounding as relaxed as he's used to from other women? Younger women.

As he casually refilled her best wine glasses, which she'd had some vaguely conscious instinct to put out, she felt the weight of the age gap between them. Her shoulders slumped as the bra dropped, and her gaze refocused to see clearly what she somehow had been unable to recognize.

I'm all boobs and belly, but his jeans are still on!

She felt a blush tingling her face, and feared that he would turn to bring the wine and see her flushed and repulsive, like a sexual nightmare.

This is unfair! No! Where's your pride?

"Saving the jeans to be a final act show-stopper?"

Too glib! Hell! Can't I do anything right?

Fear froze her again; he'd turned away from their drinks to stare and seemingly appraise all that stood before him, showing no hint of a reaction. She dared not take her eyes from on his, though he never once looked her in the eyes.

But then he said: "You're... so stunningly beautiful. I've only imagined... I mean, I can't believe that we 'are here... like this."

A warm pulse lifted her posture with relief or pride, and the blush became a sensual glow she had too rarely felt. Her mind replayed nights after Drama Society rehearsals, reliving pecked goodnight kisses in the dark. He'd never prolonged them, which she thought was due to care about her reputation, but the most vivid memory was that they were fully dressed.

Is he serious? He looks serious. So... What was that?"

"...so I didn't want to just drop my pants in case you thought all I came here for was... But, really... I feel... You know."

"Embarrassed? I'm the one who's way out of my depth. I've had only Don here... Anywhere, really... Imagine how I feel."

She read his suppressed shiver as a squirm; no other word fit, and he avoided her eyes by keeping his downcast.

Did I miss something? Is he looking for a way out?

Able to ponder her situation without his eyes' rebuke, she assessed what he saw. Bra marks on her breasts meant her waist and sides would be grooved; time would fix that, but only if he stayed. Her tummy wasn't too plump if she stood straight, but her skin looked like parchment to her, and if he came closer she was sure that would be just as obvious to him.

"See?" He said softly, still to the floor. "You can say what you think... so easily. There's something I... need to say, but I feel... like, inadequate. I don't know how to talk to such a... real woman."

He glanced up and she saw his eyes looked misty. All her emotions were too stirred up to risk speaking, and she was still trying to regain composure when he ended the silence.

"Not embarrassed...nervous. I'm trying to say that you're so much more womanly than I've ever... But now I'm here, where I've wanted to be for so long, I feel... You know. Am I making any sense at all?"

Oh, don't get me feeling all maternal. Not now!

She couldn't hold back from reaching to stroke his face. He caught her hand, and his eyes flared, but then they silently pleaded for understanding acceptance as he lowered it to the straining front of his jeans.

"See? When you kissed me I got... Any time I think of you, I get... horny. I think about you all the time."

His eyes stopped pleading and began to shine with an intensity she'd never seen. As gently as her emotions allowed, she kissed him, and as his eyelids closed they fluttered with... what, relief? It reminded her of the night she played her first role at the Drama Society and, as soon as she was backstage, she impetuously kissed him on the lips. It felt as if he'd been hoping for it, not shocked by it, but she later chided herself for acting absurdly with a boy in his mid-twenties, half her age.

And it's come to this. Just look at us... at me!

Then, his voice almost a whisper: "Helen? I've got to ask. Would you think I'm naïve... no, stupid... if I said I think I love you? Because I do...think that."

She didn't dare to speak. She let her hand offer the only possible reply: it slid the zipper of his jeans down slowly and, she hoped, sensuously enough to preserve the moment for the forever of that evening.

New Dawn

She stirred, stretching her legs and stifling a yawn. Her senses woke, quickly opening her eyes to see if it had been a dream. Evidently not; Nick's clothes were where he'd discarded them on the previously inaptly named love seat.

Bathroom? No, sounds like he's in the kitchen.

As her stretches liberated the yawn, she enjoyed recalling images from the night until she felt hair stuck to her lipstick's remnants. It got her hunting for a comb that hid in the bedside drawer's debris, and that got her thinking.

No, do it right. Brave it...face what I look like.

She crawled across the bed, smiling at memories sparked by dislodged sheets until a mirror ended that. Helen's reflection stared back at her, looking too aghast to repair makeup; her eyes locked on an image of her on hands and knees, body sagging like uncooked pastry dough. Nick knew her age, but had never seen her so vulnerably exposed; it would be cruelly obvious now, in daylight, that she is truly old enough to be his mother.

Hell! Looks like I'll find out if love is blind!

That quip in her mind eased her tension. She took his T-shirt, pulled it on, and dragged the comb through tangled remains of yesterday's expensively salon-styled hair.

"Do I hear sounds of life? I'm fixing breakfast."

"Great!" she called back. "I worked up an appetite."

Hearing buoyancy in his chuckle pleased her as much as being its cause, so Helen found some makeup to show him as radiant a face as possible. She then heard him mumble: "Umm... I left something for you.

It's down on the floor by my side of the bed."

All she saw was an eyeliner and an envelope, but then noticed writing on the envelope. As it seemed to be song lyrics her squinting eyes couldn't read, she took it back over the bed to get reading glasses from the jumbled bedside drawer.

A song? No...maybe a poem. And it's for me?

Just the idea of his writing a poem for her was so romantic that Helen was too amazed to focus on its meaning.

"Like it?"

Nick was standing in the doorway, trying to hide pride, but nothing else; he looked gloriously naked to her. Unable to say that she hadn't really read it, she offered a smile as she said: "What I'd truly like is for you to read it so I hear your rhythm in it."

"So... You do like it?"

His eyes were begging for praise, but she didn't know what to say, and masked her silence by turning her smile sultry as she handed him the poem. She saw his face flush with pride as he took the envelope, but he didn't even glance at it while softly reciting words that sounded heart-felt and already known by heart.

"Two people can always be two people;
Separated by their pasts, and the lives they lead,
And the hand-worked masks
They often choose to see themselves as being.
Two people can become one, sometimes.
They find a time when pasts and lives and masks are blurred,
And then reach out, with care, to touch and share
The precious joy of being: Being loved."

He offered a shy smile. "I called it 'Two People', but it could be 'Last Night'...as it felt to me. Although, I think it suits any couple lucky enough to share what we had... Have."

No man had ever written poetry for her, nor so freely exposed his emotions; she was speechless. Helen pulled Nick onto the bed and, as he propped on an elbow, admiring her, she peeled off his T-shirt. It was important to show him that she had learned to discard inhibitions during the night.

His gaze roved her body, an appreciative smile saying all she needed to hear as he told her: "Knowing you like what I wrote thrills me more than anything I can say!" Flushing with embarrassment, he quickly added: "Well, no... Nothing could thrill me like you are now. But I am glad you like it."

Originally published in 2015 by The New Atlantean Library
In the anthology "7 VOICES" by North Fork Writers Group

Universal Health Care

'Who am I? Where am I?' weren't philosophical queries, but first steps to gauging if he could accurately evaluate his situation. 'Who' was easy; when no one could pronounce his real name, he'd taken a perfectly English-sounding pirate's name from a book to end suspicious queries about if he was Syrian, or Somalian, or even Welsh. He felt that the name Ben Gunn would never be questioned, and it had proven to be true.

But his dark and immobilizing 'where' confused him. Ben knew that he had only to see a place to go and he could be free, but first he had to see out to that place, and then get from under something heavy. He sensed rocks in his enshrouding opaque mass, which sneezing indicated was dusty, and he felt a hard slab on his head that had a space below it in which he was breathing and sneezing. None of that explained much.

He recalled being in a war zone at the eastern end of the Mediterranean Sea to use his life-saving medical skills. Then came images of following a trail of blood from a small boy's shrapnel wounds that led via a sunlit alley into a dingy, boarded-up shop. The last thing that Ben could remember was trying to comfort the terrified child, but still not exactly where he was.

In case he was dreaming, he studied the dirt in front of him that sneeze erosion had made translucent. Seeing a shape moving behind it like a cloud shadow over a field, and linking it to sounds he now heard, he spoke, unaware his breath pushed dirt out through the pale area as he said: "People talking."

"Bubble toggly" is what two men heard as the dirt fell. Wearing United Nations Peacekeeping uniforms with Red Cross insignia; their faces wore the pain of finding bodies in debris. Robustly filthy Major Bill Delaney told relatively neat Major Nigel Knowles: "A live one to dig out... If the whole bloody heap doesn't fall. I'll go find troops to help us. Whadda ya say?"

"Anyone under this isn't likely to be in uniform," Nigel said grimly. "Army lads will shoot him on sight as a terrorist. So let's try to at least find out if it is a friend or foe first."

"He's breathin' in dirt, so now! I'll dig at the dirt spill... you keep shit up off me until I can pull 'im out. Are we go?"

Nigel knew that the pull could kill the person, but he straddled Bill's crouching body, pressed his hands against the mound and said only: "Go."

Ben felt the rubble shift as digging began, and his eyes adjusted to light as a hole formed, but all he could see was a dirty shirt. He then felt the weight pressing heavier as he heard a muffled voice yell: "I can't hold it! Hurry, Bill!"

The reply: "I'm seeing an arm I can grab, so keep holding it up!"

From inside the slowly shifting heap, Ben shocked them with: "If you get my arm free, I can assist you."

Bill replied: "I'm trying to!" Still digging, he told Nigel: "Sounds like one of you bloody Brits. Could be in your Army."

Bill had evidently moved away from the small hole to dig from another angle, because Ben could see an empty space in a room. Only he knew what ensued after his arm was freed, because falling rubble caused Bill to jump aside, toppling Nigel under a deluge of bricks. Bill turned his attention to getting Nigel out to safety, and then said: "Reckon your left arm ulna's busted, mate. Let me see what else ya did in."

"What about the poor chap buried under the wall?"

Ben's voice coming over Bill's shoulder startled them. "Thank you for your concern, but I am out now, and add to this man's view that your left side fifth rib is broken near the sternum."

Bill snarled: "I do the diagnosing, orright?"

"I am skilled in medical sciences, and–"

"And didn't examine him, so know nothing!"

"I know it will damage your lung," Ben told Nigel.

Nigel whispered: "Actually, Bill, I do have chest pains. Unlikely as it seems, the chap might be right... and a Doctor."

Bill growled: "I'll check and fix it soon as we're back at base, Nige. I'll go find our driver now." He asked softly: "Can I leave ya?"

"He is safe with me," Ben said. "Bringing medical relief to any in need is my mission here. You go, and I will see to... Nige, is it?"

"Doctor Nigel Knowles, actually. And that was Bill Delaney... a brilliant surgeon. His manner belies that pedigree, but he's Australian, so... Well... you know."

Films on TV with Australians Crocodile Dundee, Mad Max and Wolverine didn't help Ben understand Nigel's point, so he opted to say only: "I must see to your damage."

"Quite right. Supplies are in my haversack."

From a red cross-adorned bag, Ben took a tongue depressor, and exclaimed: "This is good! It is wood!"

"Get a Flexibind!" When Ben raised a cylindrical splint, Nigel added: "Now *that* is good! My broken arm will need it."

Ben shrugged and said: "I will examine that arm."

Watching Ben hold the tongue depressor in one hand and feel his arm with the other, Nigel saw the depressor snap at the moment the pain left him. He said: "Not sure how that... What you did, I mean. How is my arm?"

"Now? It is not broken. I will fit the unnecessary round splint if you insist, but first I must see to your chest."

While wondering how feeling pain vanish could be connected to a depressor breaking, Nigel felt it leave his chest as the depressor splintered when Ben touched his sternum. Rather than confront that confounding topic, he said: "From your formal speech mode, I'd say you're not actually English... but educated there. Cambridge, my ears tell me... yes? And your name is...?"

"No, English is not my first language. My name is Ben Gunn, and glad to be here to help you, Nigel. Do you feel painless now?"

"Incredibly! Damned if I saw what you did to... for me. And I absolutely want you to explain in full... But, before you do... How the hell did you get from under that wall while it was collapsing? We stopped digging as it fell on me. So...?"

Ben knew that the truth was no use; not even a fellow medician could grasp the complexities of what he had done. But he'd learned to fake explanations of what people saw as magic. "It involves the equivalent of willpower, Nigel. However it will, perhaps, be easier to understand if you know about Asian minds."

"What? Not all that mystic medicine stuff? Using meditation and incense as healing? That's not what you mean... Is it?"

"Only as it pertains to how Asian martial arts use the mind."

"Played Judo at Cambridge... I asked if you went there because I knew a few chaps like you. Bright... but a bit... odd. You know?"

Ben ignored the non sequitur detour. "I meant Karate. But if Judo taught you mind control of bodily actions, you may understand how I willed my energy to spring free as soon as I felt the load on me lighten."

A baffled Nigel had to feign understanding. "Oh... that? Timing... yes, I see...I suppose. I see you got out unscathed, too, and I am pleased for you, but... The thing is, I still don't see a connection between breaking tongue depressors and broken bones. Were mine not broken? Is it possible Bill was wrong?"

"I willed my energy to the hand holding the wood to keep the hand on you gentle," Ben lied, to keep his subterfuge-for-simplicity's-sake stratagem going.

With another facial and intellectual struggle, Nigel asked: "Asian trick? But if my bones weren't broken, why did the pain go when you touched me? Do you have... sort of healing hands... Is that it?"

Ben smiled. "I have been told that."

"Ah! So the falling bricks caused pain that your healing touch has eased and... Incredible! Tell me more back at base. Reminds me... Where the hell is Bill and our truck? Can you look?"

Ben trudged up the rubble, now remembering that he'd covered the injured boy as an explosion dropped a two-storied wall on them. He regretted having reacted too slowly in that moment, but forced his attention to staying upright while climbing the unstable rise. From its top he could see soldiers checking other crushed buildings, and was reminded that he didn't know what exploded to bury him. He called back down to Nigel: "How were all these homes destroyed?"

"Drones, of course. Most women and their kids were moved a few streets away. So civilized to tell enemies we'll be bombing hell out of them, isn't it? Damn ridiculous that two blocks east, life is allowed to go on as normal...and is doing so."

Ben said only: "I have remembered that a wounded boy I was saving is under here. He will have died. It is a tragedy."

"Yes, I hate when I patch up a kid and some fool

ruins my work. Drone... bullet... bomb... dead. I loathe
this place!"

"But there is so much work here for us, Nigel."

"Aha! I get it now. You're one of those Médecins
Sans Frontières, holier-than-thou, goody-two-shoes
Doctors! Am I right? Only such fools without borders
try to bring humanity to this hell hole."

"I cannot comprehend the concept of borders on
doctoring," Ben said. "But as I failed to save the boy, I
must go now to try to help others."

"Do you have transport? Land Rover, or similar?
If not, our truck can take you to the M-S-F hospital...
It's forty kilometres away."

With a broad grin that Ben knew couldn't be seen
from below, he said: "I can transport myself, but thank
you for the offer. I am going, so goodbye Nigel."

"Hold your I-D papers up high out there. Army lads
can be frightfully trigger-happy when they see chaps
they don't know."

Before descending to the alley, Ben said: "I thank
you for the advice, Nigel, but I have learned how to
avoid most of the trouble I encounter." Once down out
of Nigel's sight on the other side of the rubble heap, he
repeated what he'd done to escape from inside it when
he saw a place to go. Ben peered two blocks east along
a side street to where market stalls were visible, then
clicked his fingers to vanish from where he stood and
rematerialize at the market's entrance.

He saw people trying to survive as best they could,
but felt their fear, grief and misery. Sympathy for them
replaced his regret at not explaining to Nigel that the
tongue-depressor splintered as the damaged cells from
broken bones passed into it via his body. He shrugged;
no one on Earth could yet grasp how his planet's people
could mentally uplift and relocate mutated molecules
of bones or tumors to restore health.

Again determined to bring universal good health to the planet he adopted after his spacecraft's crash had marooned him, he entered the crowded market. Ben looked for any symptom of physical ailments in people; he was confident that he knew how to fix those. He also knew that he had no way to end their emotional pains. That thought triggered sad memories of being in other battle-torn villages, and they showed him that the best help he could give Earthlings would be to teach them to stop trying solve disputes with wars. From all he'd read about human history, Ben knew doing it would be the greatest test of his skills, even with his so-called magic.

WHAT MATTERS

Bam. Bam. Bam-Bam.

Duck hunters? No, handgun. Close ... Jesus! It's the school!

Bart Novak's thoughts flew to his fifteen year-old granddaughter in that school, close to where he lived; he had to call her. He stopped looking for his phone when he recalled that students handed in their phones each morning for return at day's end. When he'd heard of the school parting kids from their addictive phones, he liked the policy, but being unable to reach Rosie now had him seething with frustration. His mind registered that the nearest police base was ten miles away, so he could be first on the scene if a shooter was there...

But to do what? With what? Think!

He got his one treasure: a case that Samuel Colt had presented to an ill-fated Union officer in 1860. It held an 1851 Navy Model revolver, a gunpowder flask, percussion caps and .36 caliber lead balls. He'd owned it forty years and fired it with new powder and caps, but although not for a decade, Bart was sure it wouldn't let him down today...

Old girl's accurate. Just need one clean shot. I can do this.

Bam. Bam. Bam-Bam-Bam.

Again? That's nine now... A whole clip? Shit... go!

He put on a parka to thwart the flying sleet outside and ran to the front porch, where he pocketed all the case contained, left it on the porch and jogged on, now reviewing what he'd face...

If he reloaded... could empty it before I get off a

second shot. Load as soon as I get there... Idiot! Got no Vaseline to stop chain-fires... ah, they blow forward... so, focus. Do this right for Rosie. Really should've found my phone!

Bart assessed all the risks he could face except one: dying. At seventy, he saw each day as a bonus, albeit taxed by aging's erosion. While jogging to the school he recalled Viet Nam's deadly arsenal that he'd survived to become a husband, father, and now doting grandpa. Those thoughts ended when he saw an open side door to the school's gymnasium wing. He ran, knowing that if the school was under threat, lock-down should shut every door. He was stopped at the door by a rush of ten year-old memories of the car crash that killed his wife and son, but left the driver, his daughter-in-law, with only lingering psychological scars...

Omen I'll join them? Nah. Luck's lousy since then, but not today. Rosie needs me. Bapa's coming, babe!

He peeked into a wide hall, now breathing in gasps and seeing in freeze-frames. The door was held ajar by a woman teacher's body in a pool of blood, and beyond her were two bloody lumps that, minutes earlier, had been teenage girls...

Ah, no! But what...? Sobbing? Someone's alive.

He fought-off a need to go in before loading his gun by remembering he had read: 'Early in the Civil War, the popular Navy Colt six-shot pistol could be emptied in seconds, but reloading must have felt interminable amid hundreds of flying shots.' It haunted him as he poured gunpowder in chambers with hands too cold to control the flask's spring-release measure. As black powder spilled on the cylinder face, reviving fears of igniting a chain-fire of all chambers that could blow off the barrel, he focused on forcing balls in place with the old gun's pivot-ramrod. As his numb fingers fumbled a percussion cap on a fourth chamber's nipple, his mind was on the eerily quiet school, when...

Bam. Bam. Bam. Bam.

Fuck, no! Four loads will have to do.

Bart ran in with his gun's octagonal barrel moving side-to-side as his eyes scanned the hall to the gym's double-doors. He tried to locate the sobbing while also wondering how to fit two more caps and hold the gun ready to fire. Seeing an overturned desk hiding all but a woman's leg, he instinctively knew she was dead, but shed his boots to cross the linoleum in socks to check. He found a terrified girl of about Rosie's age with the dead woman, and tried to look calm as he whispered: "You're safe. What's your name? This a teacher?"

"It's Missus Schultz... I'm Jess." Through a sob, she added: "Saved... me under the desk, and kept Greg..."

He deduced from blood in a chair that brave Mrs. Schultz had died in it, but had to ask: "Who's Greg?"

A lanky youth slid from behind an overturned chair to hug Jess as he said: "Me. He didn't shoot me."

"So you saw the shooter?" Greg nodded. "One?" Another nod. "Know him?" Both kids shrugged. "See a gun or guns?"

As Jess shook her head, Greg said: "Two pistols. Maybe. One in his belt. Well, I saw something there as he reached under his hoodie. It's black. His jeans, too. He seemed to have lots of ammo clips in his pockets."

Shit! No matter... I won't survive a fire fight!

"Good to know. But do you know where he went?"

Greg pointed to the gym's doors. "Took four senior girls, and...none came out. I just heard four shots."

Ah, no! Why pull four aside? Where is everyone else? And why is it so... deathly quiet?

Bart limited his questions to: "Another way out?"

"Fire exits," Greg said. "But none opened. An alarm goes off... unless there's a game on. And you can hear that everywhere."

"So, as far as we know, he's in the gym... Right?"

Greg nodded, but said: "Or in its change rooms, or their shower rooms. Or Coach Kemprowski's office. No, it'll be locked. Equipment room should be, too. So that's the gym and five side rooms... plus the office."

Oh, great! Ambush Alley! Got to get these kids out.

Bart smiled reassuringly. "Hear the siren? Help's coming, but I'll need a plan of the gym rooms." As Greg drew on a page of the teacher's scattered papers, Bart said: "You two run over the road and hide on that brick house's porch till the cops get here. But first... where could Rosie... Rosemary Novak be?"

Jess said: "Room two B. Ro's in my class. I should be there, but I was late and... Missus Schultz was–"

"Yeah, thanks. Now, go... both of you. Fast if that gym alarm goes off." He smiled to soften that scare, and watched them run by the three bodies, but when Greg turned back at the doorway, Bart hissed: "Scram!"

"No, Mister, you should know... I think the guy was upstairs, where Ro's room two B is. So if you're Ro's granddad, I hope you find her... and she's... okay."

"Thanks. Go!"

Should've asked if the first shots were upstairs!

Bart was torn; find Rosie, or the shooter. A phone on the floor offered an option to call 911. Getting no dial tone led him to notice no lights were on and wonder if the power and phones had been disabled...

Should've found my phone! Where are the cops?

He assumed the power was cut and decided to find the shooter before police arrived, but had to review...

This four and four girls dead? Fired thirteen shots, so he fitted a new clip. Hold tight, Rosie... Bapa's here.

Bart went on, watching for movement inside glass panels of the gym's doors, and checked Greg's sketch before opening one door. He slid inside, tried another useless light switch and hurried to the wall Greg had marked with an equipment room and boys' changing rooms. He only then glanced fully around...

That's the office opposite...with glass walls! Be dead if he was there... Don't freak out...just go!

Staying near the wall to be unseen from the rooms on his side, he held the gun up to fire, but not cocked to avoid the metallic triple-click sound in the silence.

Stay cool. One chance against an automatic.

Finding the equipment room locked turned his focus to the change rooms on opposite sides of the gym. Farther along, at an arch to a lateral hall that blocked a view into the boys' room, he tightened his thumb on the gun's hammer. Straining his senses, Bart realized that a noise he thought was rain was water splashing in the girls' room, opposite him...

Can I turn my back on over there to go in? Where is everyone? And where's the old gung-ho me?

Holding in breath to be quiet and keep his nerve, he slid into the hall and, finding it empty, entered the dim room and shower room; both empty. After that, at the girls' room, Bart crept to the end of its lateral hall and could hear whimpering amid the noise of showers running and sleet lashing windows...

If he's facing my way in, he sees me. Other way, the crier could see me and react. Ah, won't matter.

He entered at the back of a man in black holding a gun down at his side and facing a naked teenager with her head down, too afraid or embarrassed to look up. Bart doubted if the lead ball could go through the man into her, but knew that killing him could prevent police from learning his motive.

Don't overthink it! Get the prick!

As he reached out, pulled the man's hood back into a choke hold, Bart cocked the gun and pressed its barrel into the neck behind the right ear as he said: "Freeze! Or I'll blow your fucking head off! Drop that gun!"

"No." That syllable was arrogant. "I'll blow you up with this slut. I'm wearing pounds of explosives, and I'm ready and willing to detonate it."

No second gun Greg saw under the hoodie... a fucking suicide vest! Jesus! Will he do it? Chance it.

Bart tilted the gun and fired; the ball tore through the man's ear and along the cheek, burning it in the gunpowder's flash. The girl's terrified shriek and the man's howl of pain became a multi-pitched screech.

Don't make me kill you, Bart thought, but said: "You're dead next shot, but no virgins up there will like your face now. So keep that gun pointing down."

Despite his searing wounds, the man was able to say: "This isn't stupid towel-head Allah crap! I have a manifesto to tell–"

Bart snapped: "On you to blow up too? Doubt it."

Got him! Didn't plan that. Will he risk blowing up without leaving his record of why? Push him.

"So keep your gun pointing down, as it is, and–"

Running footsteps grew loud entering the room, along with a louder male voice. "Police! Drop the gun, or I'll shoot."

"Wait! He's the one you want," Bart said as calmly as he could. "Armed, and says he's in a suicide vest."

And not a bit fazed by a face bleeding like a stuck pig.

As neither the officer nor the terrorist seemed to know what to do, Bart asked: "You got back-up?"

"Four cars are on the way. But who's asking? Who put you in charge?"

"Me. Marines Lieutenant. I can do this so no one dies."

Best he can't see my Colt. Keep his eyes on this prick.

Bart stood closer to the terrorist's back to conceal his old gun as he said: "Get a bead on him from his left side. Girl, get your clothes and wait outside! And you, feller...stay cool, and let's at least be civil. I'm Bart Novak. You?"

The officer queried: "Not never-sober-Novak... the local drunk?"

Bart ignored him; the terrorist was saying: "No one will remember either of you after one news cycle. Four precocious sluts may keep up T-V's ratings for a while, but Kevin McCoy's name will be long remembered."

Bart was thinking: *Ego freak* as the officer snarled: "Crap! What'll be on T-V is Officer Mike Kelly nabbed a mad killer. So don't even think of movin', dickhead!"

As they traded insults, Bart's mind registered their absurdity, and that both had Irish heritage and similar ages, but were as different as imaginable...

McCoy's tough... face must feel on fire, but he's not bitching. Ready to die? Kelly'll help him without a care for what this is all about. Thinking of Kelly took Bart's mind to: *Lose my wife and boy and go on a two-year bender... the world knows. Rarely drink since... and no bastard notices.*

As the young officer moved by, Bart said: "Gun's in his right hand, Kelly. What's in his left? Where is it?"

"Nothing. Hand's in front of his... Aw, Jesus... Did he jerk-off all over that chick? Whadda scumbag!"

McCoy said superciliously: "You're sordidly stupid. I had her feel unbearable humiliation, like she and her evil coterie inflicted on me. The others are showering off their sins...and blood. My manifesto tells why. And, so you know, my left hand holds a wire to a detonator. One tug...boom!"

Bart said: "First, tell me... How'd you get them so quiet? And spike the lights and phones? Impressive."

Can't easily put a hand with a gun or wire in a pocket for papers. It may be a thumb drive... harder to get out with a full hand... Shit... what's he saying?

"...Masters in Electronics." McCoy's arrogance was palpable. "I rigged explosives on doors. Now it won't matter, I'll tell you... most just look real to stop them

113

being opened while I got the herd in the auditorium. Fear of bombs keeps them quiet. My manifesto states my aims, but what's impressive is how I improvised on my plan today... I impressed myself!"

Kelly snapped: "Impressive? With two guns on ya? You're just a fucked up geek... who fucked this right up!"

McCoy's response: "It's no wonder cops are called dumb pigs. If I'm shot, I fall... pulling this wire... and it's bye-bye piggy."

Bart recognized he was lucky that his shot didn't cause McCoy's hand on the wire to jerk and detonate his bomb, but he said: "Hold it, Mike. I'd sure like to know what Mister McCoy's plan was before I die. Let's hear him out."

Talk...brag...whatever. I have bombs to consider.

Over the sound of sirens, McCoy did brag of all he did. Bart's mind was busy, but he heard the snippets: "...office staff first ...baskets of cell phones, now under bombs ...teachers obeyed, reminded their job's to keep kids safe ...too afraid to leave with auditorium doors bomb-rigged ...found those four bitches and brought them here ...she ran as I shot the others, but you know I caught her." Bart then heard: "Manifesto explains it all, but enough talk. I'll let you... Novak, take it away to safeguard for posterity."

"I thank you for sparing me. In return, Mike and I will lower our guns... after you let go that wire. We'll point ours at the floor, like yours is, while you get out your manifesto."

Kelly snarled: "Waste o' time! One shot'll end it."

"Want to die, Mike? He has enough explosives on him to bring down the roof! Not that we'd know... we'll be all over the walls by then. Right, Mister McCoy?"

Just say yes...don't go spouting-off again.

McCoy simply nodded, so Bart gestured at Kelly to do nothing and said: "Sirens just stopped...time's up.

Those cops will come charging in, armed and angry. Mister McCoy's issue, Mike, is that he has to let go the wire to give me his manifesto, but he has to know he can do it without worrying about you."

McCoy said: "But why should I trust you, Novak?"

"Because I agree... whatever your reason is for this, it must be told... made public. I mean... I assume you'll explain about the girls and all the dead. Three here in the showers, and four I saw at the side entrance..."

McCoy's head slumped. "Ah, them... You'll have to add that, Novak. All I wanted was the four evil bitches... See, after I rounded up everyone and got the sluts here, it got chaotic with two teachers and some kids. I told them to stay still, but they'd heard my gun. So with a teacher already yelling in a cell and running to the door and the other trying a desk phone... Why have a desk blocking a hall? Crazy. Anyway... what else could I do?"

Stay cool. And credible.

"They were calling cops... I get it. But... two dead kids with them?"

"They surprised me. I thought a boy there might try to play hero, but it was those girls who tried to take my gun away."

"More reason to get your manifesto out to explain it. Ah, hear that noise? Cops. They'll hear you took four girls this way and be in no mood to talk when they get here. So let go the wire and get out your manifesto. And Mike! Do... nothing! Just back off a few steps and keep your gun pointed down."

Kelly slid back, lowering his Glock, so Bart raised his gun from McCoy's neck and held it up high, which McCoy couldn't see because he kept his eyes on Kelly. As McCoy's left hand, without a wire, reached around for a back pocket, Bart slammed the heavy old Colt's butt onto his head, dropping an instantly unconscious McCoy to the floor.

"We did it!" Kelly kept howling amid his laughs and leaping about. "So much for snotty nerds!"

We? Okay, but just keep on celebrating.

Exploiting Kelly's inattention, Bart took a wad of pages from McCoy's pocket and put it and the Colt in his parka. He heard police in the hall and felt a rush of fatigue after the few minutes of stress, so he shut his eyes and slumped on a bench. His mind saw images of men with explosives that ranged from improvised to sophisticated; he's seen them in films, and on corpses. He saw those when he had led his men at tunnels to where Viet Cong fled, or staged ambushes, or made booby-traps, or slept, and often died.

Can't stay here...must find out if Rosie's okay.

The thought arose just as he heard men clumping into the room to be met by Officer Kelly's: "We're good here. I got him on the floor. Just cuffed his hands behind him."

Bart opened his eyes, but didn't move until the babble of talk subsided and a man asked: "Who's the old guy on the bench? He part of this?"

"No, sir," Kelly replied respectfully, identifying the man in a Kevlar-vest as the group's senior officer. "He's one of us... local. He, like... helped me."

Bart rose and strode to them, a hard gaze at Kelly unnerving the young officer while he shook hands with the group leader, saying: "Lieutenant Novak, retired... But glad to help Mike. I know you want a debrief, but my grandkid is here somewhere and I need to let her know I am too and she's safe. I'll be back after I do that." He didn't wait for a response.

~ ~ ~ ~ ~ ~ ~ ~ ~ ~ ~ ~ ~

At six o'clock that evening, Bart entered the house he'd lived in for eight years and was met by his best friend and landlord, Pete Wilton. They'd survived life in tandem since school; both served in Viet Nam and both lost wives, but Pete found Anna and remarried to become more content than most of the Nam Vets they knew. The couple saved Bart after his wife and son died; drink cost Bart his job at a time when even sober sixty year-olds weren't hired, and foreclosure of his home put him on the streets, a destitute drunk. They'd taken Bart in, helped re-build the man everyone once respected, and were glad to have him in their life. The old pals were again so close that they could sense each other's moods, and read the thoughts behind them.

Pete said: "Heard you were at the school...must've been hell." His eyes tightened. "What happened, Bart? Talk to me... Look like you need to. Get wasted after?"

Irritation etched Bart's weary sigh, but he looked composed saying: "First... No, didn't drink, but I need one now! Any of that good whisky left? Glen...kinky?"

Pete laughed. "Glenkinchie... and well deserved. Talk while I pour. Anna's got roast lamb for you..." He paused to call to the kitchen: "Honey, have Bart and I got time to talk a while?"

As Bart slumped in his usual chair, Anna entered, removing an apron from her Earth-Mother hips and pulling an old flip-phone from its pocket. After kissing Bart, she scolded: "You didn't have your cell! We were at my doctor's and I called to find out what was going on... Everyone was talking about some trouble at the school. I tried again when I got home and heard your phone in here... it was under your chair's cushion." She handed the phone to Bart. "A fat lot of use this was! Anyhow... I'll give you both ten minutes to talk... then I want you to tell it all over again at dinner."

After a sip of Scotch, Bart began by describing the need he'd felt to keep Rosie safe after hearing the first shots. With Pete continuing to refill their glasses, his account evolved to be as crisp as reports he had made after patrols in Viet Nam. He was describing how he'd implied that he was a retired police officer so he could escape from the gym before the real police started to ask him questions, when Pete interjected.

"Wait! You took the guy's manifesto? Can I read it?"

"Gave it to the top cop. Not the one I conned... his boss arrived some time before I got back there."

"I heard you might've left and gone back. And that you were with cops... maybe arrested ...maybe drunk. No one knew why else you'd be there. I'll drain this bottle for us... you fill in your story."

"Not much more to tell. A teacher took me to Rosie, but guess what? I found her calming scared friends. Cool as ice, she said: 'Hi, Bapa, hear the news?' Then she asked, like it couldn't possibly be true: 'You didn't come for me? We were fine... That crazy guy was mad about some senior girls.' That's my grandkid, Pete. She's some amazing kind of cool!"

"So... what? You left her there? After all that?"

"Sure. She was obviously fine, and I had shit to do."

"Like... read the manifesto? What the hell did it say?"

"Five pages of writing so tiny I couldn't read a word of it. Shrinks say tiny script shows you're fucked in the head. But maybe that's only as true as people who say shootings at schools prove we should lock-up loonies and arm teachers, while others say no one would ever be shot if all guns were banned."

Pete asked: "You went back and learned...what?"

Bart pondered that briefly. "Not much. I went to give a statement... like a witness, and pretty much got away with it. That young idiot, Kelly, had bragged on and on about how he was the one who captured McCoy and saved the last girl."

Pete had to ask: "It's dark now... your statement took all day? And you didn't say why you left and went back. So...?"

"Had to...I shot McCoy's ear and dented his skull with a museum piece that's more valuable to me than its money worth. It was too obvious that Kelly didn't fire... Procedure is to check police guns. If I'd thought fast, maybe I'd have said Kelly had my gun and did it all. One flaw in that is I doubt he could stick to the story in the investigation this is sure to get... Top Brass cops, politicians and the media all over it. Right?"

Pete nodded. "So you just had to 'fess-up and face the consequences? So... what happened? Surely they didn't grill you all fucking day?"

"Nah. My old Colt's unlicensed. I couldn't have it confiscated, so I lied. The top cop knew it was bullshit, but wouldn't drop a veteran my age in shit... not after he knew I did all that Kelly said he'd done. So he and I agreed on a story that lets me keep my gun and get no publicity... Kelly gets all the glory. See?"

"That cop helped you spin it that way? What's the hell sort of story did you come up with?"

Bart chuckled. "Before I met him, I'd come here to get your air pistol. I said I'd used it and that cop didn't argue, though he'd seen the mess I made of McCoy's face. He put the air gun in an evidence bag that won't get near a trial. They've got McCoy, his gun, bombs and manifesto... He's toast. And if they lose your gun..."

"I won't be able to ping squirrels on the bird feeder. Big deal. But don't you want to know why he wanted to kill those four girls? I sure do."

"Watch T-V news. We already know the world's full of pricks wanting to kill as jihadists, revolutionaries, to revenge humiliation, or just get a kick out of shooting cats. Kill-crazies are all the same... and we saw in Nam that all we can do is stop them before they do too much harm. And saw that there's no end to crazy pricks." Bart paused before: "Nam taught us to trust our instincts. Mine said that his booby-traps were fake...he wanted to scare everyone so they didn't try to stop him doing what he went there to do. He's crazy, for sure, but I have to admit that he planned all this brilliantly."

Pete grinned. "Seems so. But were your instincts right about it?"

"Sort of. The bomb squad said that stuff wired to doors looked the real McCoy...their pun that I'm going to use ...but those amazingly good looking fakes had no detonators or triggers." Bart chuckled. "Ah, getting old fucks memory. I said I didn't learn much, but I know the fake explosives were made on a Three-D printer... so McCoy's not just an educated arrogant prick... He must be rich to have his own Three-D printer at home."

Pete suggested: "Or maybe used one at wherever he works?"

"Who would risk printing bombs in an office? But, again, it doesn't matter how pricks do shit. The world's lousy with kill-crazies who can get real... or just plain old scary-looking, weapons. We have to do more than just beat them down... We have to do it in ways that won't fuck-up of who we are and how we live."

"Getting philosophical to counter-balance losing your memory, Bart?"

"Ha! But you know what we saw in Nam... and its impact on us there and here. Still, we knew we fought to keep our pals alive. That's a world away in time and distance. My world's tiny now. Gwen and Rick left it ten years ago. His Meg went a sort of crazy I can't handle and found a boring fart, who Rosie says is good for her. I burned every friend except... See? You two and Rosie are what matter in my world now... and I was there for one of you today. And I saw Rosie in her world. Taking charge... helping her pals. I felt... feel so proud."

Pete smiled at his old pal. "You showed Rosie how much you care. I bet she's as proud that you were there just for her."

Bart sighed wearily. "She might never know what I did. Only you know the whole story. Well, all except…"

Should I say? It'll come out. So better tell Pete.

"There's this. McCoy did have a suicide vest… a real one. He was prepared to die… just had to pull the wire to break the contact. I would've never seen Rosie, Anna and you again. Imagine."

What a lousy way to die… not knowing why. But, then again, who does?

HIS COMFORT

Pierre Bondi left the cemetery manager's office thanking... whatever the fuck he said his name was, for revising the paperwork as he had requested. He also waved a cemetery map to confirm that he could find the graves as he strode along the plush-pile hall to the exit, savoring the ambient silence until his pulling on the polished brass knob turned his attention to...

Shit... fingerprints. Should clean them before I put more outside. No, remember... Graeme would say I'm being O-C again. And tell me cleaners do it daily to keep the brass shiny. And that new shrink... Roberta, she'd say the same. Well, fuck it... it's messy.

After cleaning the doorknob with one of his many Kleenex, Pierre closed the door without touching its outer handle, but wiped it anyway. Before moving on, he checked the map's zig-zagging red line toward his destination, a rectangle of four numbered plots filled by red ink. Glad that Mister whatever-the-fuck-name's ink stayed within the lines, and sure that he knew the way, he left the office's foliage façade. At Wisteria Walk he paused to gaze over a garden of pleasingly uniform yellow roses to the crematorium chapel, where friends too-often arrived in caskets. Now glad that his parents had left acceptably precise instructions for burial in the neighboring plots marked red on the map, Pierre again started walking towards them.

His reason for the map, which he had dismayingly creased while reliving funerals, was to memorize the names of roads and paths. His reason to do that was to be able to tell Graeme all about the day. He'd stopped visiting his mother's grave long ago for reasons he now defined as Painful-And-Pointless.

Yes, right at Rose Of Sharon Road through ugly Irish headstones that make Italian monuments to bad taste look bland. Graves should be... Ah, not the day to think about it... only what to show Graeme, and... Shit! Camera? Yes... jacket pocket. Now, left on Primrose Path. How could I forget?

A few zigs and zags later, Pierre stood staring at his parents' intricately interlocked marble headstones that his father designed. His mind was seeing episodes from his life. He tried to recall having fun with his big sister Belle when their father was away on work projects that Pierre had never understood. Nor, for that matter, had ever known why anyone would hire such a relentlessly pedantic consulting engineer with zero tolerance for even the slightest imperfection.

No wonder I'm fucked in the head. If he'd stayed a consultant and stayed away I might be able to learn how to pose as normal.

Jacques Bondi was promoted beyond his level of competence, called the Peter Principle of management; the Pierre Principle of foul fathering, said his son. As an office-bound boss, Jacques had micro-managed so abusively he was forced to retire early to prevent mass resignations by his staff. So he consulted from home, making his two kids' lives hell and his wife, Joanne, an alcoholic. Belle had fled to college, but took the Bondi dysfunction gene along with her; insecurity and all her personal flaws crippled her studies and love life.

Poor Belle. As fucked up as I am, but lonely too. If she knew then what we do now she'd have killed the old bastard for what he did to Ma. Let alone for the shit we got.

Pierre got out his camera, but couldn't photograph the grave; he couldn't tear his gaze from Jacques Paul Bondi's intimidating name. All it represented haunted him, most especially Belle's troubles, like Jacques' rage when she got pregnant at college. Their father saw it as the ultimate sin of being life-divertingly stupid. The father of Belle's kid was a victim of her neediness, and he stayed only until the marriage exposed her cocaine habit. A judge put the kid in the care of his father; both instantly vanished and hadn't been seen since.

Belle remarried, but it ended woefully. She said her husband molested their daughters, but Pierre wasn't surprised by the girls telling a Divorce Court Judge that they wanted to live with their Dad. Belle later said that had made her a non-active lesbian, which to Pierre was an excuse for a life alone with no commitments. Since then, she'd contacted him only by email, but a written note recently listed her end-of-life wishes as cremation, with her ashes to feed a rose garden. An underlined P.S. noted: "Don't dare put me in the plot Pa bought for me, Little Bro, or I'll haunt you forever in yours!"

Stop reliving this shit! Too much to do, and time's getting away. But where to start? Maybe a first shot showing the span of what were to be Belle's and my plots either side of their graves. Don't over-think it!

Pierre took wide-shot photos from all angles before he tightened the framing to get the front and both sides of the four-plot area. He then took a sheaf of gladiolus from an obviously well-tended grave nearby, put it on the plot beside his father's grave, and took a photo of its proximity to Jacques' headstone. He wanted to take more, but couldn't; Pierre burst into tears that refused to stop pouring out decades of suffering and all of his hatred for the man in the grave.

Why couldn't you just shut up and accept it when you heard I'm gay? So it shocked and embarrassed you... So what? Just you being you embarrassed Belle and me! But you didn't even notice our anguish! I can shrug-off being fucked up by you, but I'll never forgive how you bullied mom into this way-too-early grave. I'll hate you as long as I live for that, and if there is an afterlife, you'll know how that fucking feels!

Pierre's mind was in turmoil, swirling all the angst he'd felt. Nothing he did satisfied Jacques, even before his teenage emergence as an un-flamboyant gay, when his father refused to speak to him, or let his mother even say his name after Pierre left home. His escape to college and law school was possible only because of an effort-rewarded bursary and his mother's inheritance, which should have financed her life free from Jacques. Feeling responsible for trapping her in that offensive marriage was a pain that had never faded, but flared up at times like Jacques' response to his son's graduation from Law School: "Lawyers are blights on life, so that little shit will fit right in!"

What did you know? Nothing about my work! Ma would've loved to tell you about my pro bono work for women's shelters. She was so proud of me for that. But you never let her, or asked one time about what I was doing. Oh, no... You couldn't let anything like a fact in to spoil your image of me... the useless fairy.

And then there was Graeme, who was a partner at the firm where Pierre first became an Associate. They'd now been together for thirty years as lovers, and half of that as partners in their own well-respected law office. Jacques had never accept his son's life or the happiness it had brought him. Pierre didn't resent that as much as his mother having been able to see him with Graeme only at impromptu restaurant lunches if Jacques was busy. Perhaps even more than that, he was still pained by her having died before the law change that allowed them to wed, not that Jacques would have let her go to the service if she'd been alive. The swirl in his mind coalesced to show how his life was now reduced to having dead parents, a who-knew-where big sister who chose to avoid him, and the love of his life wasting away at a frighteningly fast pace in a hospice.

I'll be there soon, Grae-babe, with a map and able to tell you all the walkways I took to get here. And I'll show you pics of where you will be until I'm beside Ma, and then we'll laugh about you lying with this prick who cruelly darkened our life by never accepting that we're alive. Imagine it, love... eternally laughing at how you being there will never let him rest in peace. I'll take great comfort from that.

Paranoia In Private

The guests at Kim Haisin's recent fortieth birthday party included his peers among Singapore's elite global financiers. All knew his charm and generosity, but little of his private life, and some believed he was hiding his lineage. He didn't look Chinese, Malay, or Indonesian, and gossip had his mother a Malay-Indian, which could mean British seeds in his family tree had spawned his vaguely Caucasian looks. Colleagues were as intrigued by Kim never taking extra time at clients' expense on trips to New York, Zurich or London; he left Singapore only reluctantly and always returned promptly.

No Singaporean knew that his mother had changed their names on arriving from Australia in 1985 to stay with family until her husband let her know they could return. All Kim knew about it was that his father was an Australian Army Major, and his mother had never received the message. For thirty years, she'd refused to discuss it, but Kim deduced that she believed Major Allan Hayes died on a secret government mission, and that had somehow led to Luli Hayes, née Sharma, and her ten year-old son Keith becoming Luan and Kim Haisin. Through Kim's life, his mother had frequently insisted that they must live as those names: "Always... No exceptions... Ever!"

Kim's past haunted him today on his return from her funeral, feeling the emptiness of his affluent life. He'd obeyed his mother's wishes by not inviting a soul to the service, or publishing an obituary. Memories had him feeling alone and so resentful of his father that he needed Single Malt Scotch, and lots of it, to flood the void now expanding within him.

Entering his penthouse, he confronted the sterility of his life; its walls of investment value works of art had no balance of personal photos or mementoes. Like Kim in his Armani suits, Chanel ties and Gucci shoes, it was elegantly adorned, but felt sterile. Not that anyone ever visited; Kim and his mother let in only the long-serving staff of twin sister housemaids, Lin and Lan, chef Mei, and Kim's Eurasian driver, Ron.

At a rack of Scotches, his only medium for escapes from life, he pulled an old Balvenie to drown ice in a glass, and went out to his roof patio to let a view of the marina relax him. Inner turmoil and humidity ruined any hope of that, so Kim retreated to air-conditioning and drank beside a table with an array of mementoes he found in his mother's apartment, seemingly hidden in closets. As they held better memories than all that blighted his day, he studied them. Two photos he had thought lost were now in a silver dual-frame. One was of him as nine year-old Keith in a Sydney suburban backyard, and he could remember the home, but not which parent took the photo.

Kim knew he took the other of his mother with a man's arm on her shoulder; he'd taken it to school to explain his odd skin and eyes to Aussie kids. That arm was his only image of his father; his mother said they'd be returning to Australia, so they had only pictures that were in their wallets. Seeing them again now, his often refilled glass had him feeling emotions he rarely let surface; long-standing barricades against the pain of the past fell and he felt tears welling.

The photo of his mother's pretty young face and happy smile ignited a need to talk to her. For intimacy to say all that he felt he had to, he slid the picture from the frame to hold it. A wad of paper fell to the floor as he did; being too intent on speaking to her to really see it, he dismissed it as padding.

"I've always done my best for you, Mama. But you wanted Dad... and never said why he was so special. All I knew was that he left us. But please know I'll stay who you wanted... needed me to be. I'm promising to always be your Kim, Mama. Please know that, and rest easy. I will always love... and respect you."

He rose to get ice for another refill, and felt the effects of the Scotch on his balance. After a deep breath, he let his mother's discipline training of him restore his focus by neatly lining-up all the items he'd found in her closets. To return the silver dual-frame to the table, he had to retrieve the fallen padding. It was paper of the flimsily brittle sort once used in Air Mail to lower cost, a memory he reflected on until he saw type on it. Now sure his mother hid the papers in the frame, Kim tried to see why and found a transcript of a meeting with a doctor on which his father had written explanations.

DICTAPHONE TAPE – 1
Monday, 3rd December, 1984 – Office of DR Ron Franks & DR Judith Harris – Mount Street, North Sydney

Just ME & DR Judi. Ron in Hunter Valley buying a winery – me dying no priority for him! Turned on recorder in pocket as Judi got Specialist's report..

DR: Prognosis isn't good. Sorry.

ME: So what now? *No response. She read blood test results and Specialist's letter – as if to stall.*

DR: This phase can last a while, so I see no need to rush you into hospital. *Glanced at me and back to letter.*

ME: You do not know for sure?

DR: You are Ron's patient. He will check with Dr Rosen, the Specialist, when he is back.

ME: So what are the prescriptions you gave me for?

DR: To stabilize symptoms. All you should feel for a while is tiredness, so no exertion. And avoid stress.

ME: Easy for you to say. But seriously. What am I facing? The truth, Judi. *Tried to smile through this.*

DR: Marrow transplants. No problem, usually, but Dr Rosen notes that you need special treatment for those rare blood abnormalities the tests found.

ME: Sounds bloody expensive.

DR: From this, it seems it might be. Rosen recommends that we refer you to a London colleague of his.

ME: Is that Doc out here now?

DR: I read this as you go to him. *Avoided eye contact.*

ME: And stay to be treated? My health fund will not pay for that, will it?

DR: In the UK? I doubt it. Ron will ask Rosen when he talks to him. Or the UK Specialist. Brian McLachlan. *Looked like she didn't want to answer honestly.*

ME: If it is NO, I am fucked! Sorry Judi. *She ignored swearing & tried for a hopeful expression.*

DR: It must be from defoliants you were exposed to in Vietnam, so your costs could be covered or subsidised by some ex-servicemen's fund.

ME: Government backed out long ago! Lots of Nam vets have leukemia or cancer from that shit, but our only way to get help is a TV fund for us as charity cases. Not me! So I need the cost of treatment in England.

DR: I will talk to Ron about it all, including the financing. For now, let us hope there is a less expensive option locally. *Stood to go to door - looked glad to end meeting.*

ME: I sure hope! But until we know it all,

this stays with you, me and Ron. Right? Not
a word to Luli.

DR: Of course. But she will have to know
soon, Allan.

ME: So I keep taking the pills until I
hear from Ron or you, right? *Changed topic to ease up
on Judi.*

Having found nothing to explain why his mother
hid it, other than her usual obsession for privacy, Kim
assessed its clues to his parents. The little he knew of
their marriage told him that if she knew of this illness
she wouldn't have left Australia. As the letter must have
come to her in Singapore, he had to wonder: *Did she
get any other letters or papers, and still have them?*

He found another transcript behind the frame's
other photo. Its tone was harsher, prompting Kim to
re-read the pages carefully.

DICTAPHONE TAPE – 2
Wednesday, 9th January, 1985 – Office of
P. Balff (MD MSP PhD) – Roslyn Gardens,
Elizabeth Bay

Just ME & Pieter Balff (Psychiatrist)
*Cartoons show patients lying on a couch but room's sleek chairs
looked sterile. Painting of 2 red squares on a wall. No diploma.*

DOC: Come on in, Major Hayes.

ME: Just Mister these days.

DOC: Some of my visitors are not yet used
to civilian life or like using their title.
Either way, it helps to get chats going if I
show respect for their past.

ME: Visitors? *Could not let him get away with that!*

DOC: A friendlier way of thinking of them,
is it not?

ME: No, it is bullshit. We are patients.
This is no less a Shrink's hideout by having
visitors and no couch.

DOC: Ha! The old couch cliché.

I felt sorry for him, dealing with blokes like me, but his job was fixing war neurosis so I expected a case-hardened Doc. I hated having to see a Shrink for doing my duty, but tried a smile. He laughed - an OK tactic when stuck for words, but his laugh was as phony as my smile, so we were getting nowhere.

ME: Heard the old couch cliché so often you can no longer crank up a proper laugh?

Did try to keep it light, but anger was making me snide.

DOC: Mister Hayes. Allan. May I call you Allan?

ME: Yeah. Why not? *Looked like he needed to.*

DOC: It might help you to see me not as a psychiatrist, but as a counselor who offers you advice.

ME: Do I need advice?

DOC: We all do at times. Hearing your prognosis was traumatic. Your mind must come to terms with it. It is my job to help you to find options, if that is what you need. Or just be here to talk to.

ME: I say enough in swearing for us both. It does not help to stop me stewing about the death sentence they dropped on me.

DOC: Allan, listen. You have to- *Looked rattled – I cut in.*

ME: You listen! I am not usually this shitty. I was The Iceman in the Army. You have your job, but I have the leukemia they say is a rare form I have one chance in ten fucking thousand of surviving!

DOC: I understand. I read the file and am an MD. That helps in this practice, but - I am sorry.

ME: Are you? My one chance is a year in an English clinic. If I live that long. I ask if my medical fund covers it, they say 'sorry'. Everybody says that! It will cost about a million bucks. Who the fuck has that?

Not an ex-Army Major!

It got awkward. He patted my shoulder, but I hate sympathy. It must have showed - he looked lost again, so I kept going.

ME: I am not shitty because trying to cure Leukemia costs more than I have. And dying from Agent Orange in Nam is no different to going by a mine or bullet. While the government fucking us does not surprise me, my Asian wife and our pale yellow boy face bigotry here when I die. And if I get money to go to England, but die there, they will be broke. So I am shittier than other blokes who come in here. Get it?

He did not answer. He sat there watching me rant. Maybe he had heard it all before, so knew to show no emotion. But he knew I would not visit again. I would sort it out my way - somehow.

When Kim had absorbed both documents, queries filled his mind. He'd learned almost as much about his father from the pages as he ever did from his mother. It distressed him to only now know of his father's fatal disease, but he felt worse about his mother not learning of it until she'd settled in Singapore with orders to lay low here until she could go back to Australia.

Kim's attention went to a note on the top of the first set of papers. With an ultra-sharp pencil, his father had written: *Luli-love – This happened before the Fed Cops recruited me. I wish I could have spared you from this and all that other stuff. Al xxxxxxxxxxxx*

Kim could not know what 'other stuff' meant until he learned more, but the letters had him hyper-actively alert to oddities, and one example of odd was a broken underline of the X kisses. With the aid of a magnifying glass he was able to see tiny lettering: *see back note.* He saw no note until a magnified view of what looked to be pencil lines on the back of a page showed even smaller words that were too tiny to read. He wondered if his mother saw them, and recalled that she had once asked to use his computer's magnifying scanner. Kim used it and was able to read many of the words, but some were blurred, probably by his mother's hands.

An emptied pot of coffee later, all the legible words were in his computer, with gaps for the blurs. It made sense only after he saw *RSL* as *Returned Servicemen's League*. Deciphering that and *AO* brought a grasp of what his father wrote, and Kim typed a summary rather than try to deduce the missing words.

Agent Orange = Dad's leukemia / many Aussies in Vietnam got ill / Gov blamed for not warning re USA's AO / secret RSL meetings agree to prove problem's size & help families / ex-soldiers to record experiences as proof / Dad did these 2 reports.

Apparently, his father sent the pages to tell his wife of his disease, and the pencil notes told her he'd joined others to force Australia's Government to compensate the families. As Kim hit 'Print', he noticed 4:45 on his computer screen, the time his chef left home to come and cook dinner for him and, until now, his mother. He sent a text: *Dine with me PLEASE?* Seconds later, Kim saw: *OK*. Before returning to his Scotch, he turned to his keyboard and added to the on-screen page:

WHEN did she get these? / Are these ALL she got? / If not, WHERE are others / WHY didn't I know about all this?

~ ~ ~

Cho Mei was about to tell her son Xin-Yi that she was leaving when her phone chimed the tone she'd set for Kim Haisin's texts. Mei replied before she realized what his invitation to dine with him would entail. It was more plea than request; he needed to be comforted after his mother's funeral.

Mei saw Luan's death impacting her life more than she liked to face; Kim paid her big salary and benefits to buy loyalty to his mother and him. Mei didn't know what he did for Lin and Lan, or his driver, Ron, but saw they protected the Haisins' privacy by never discussing their employers' lives. Mei had no idea if the others knew anything about what Luan told her when Kim was away and his mother needed a diversion from extra anxiety. She never knew if Luan's not referring to their gin-fueled chats indicated no memory of them, or the shame of having hinted at too much, most particularly the reasons for her thirty years of isolation.

Despite these complexities, Mei had loved her now twelve years with the Haisins. Kim's maid Lin, whom she knew from school, introduced her to him as the chef he needed, aware her old friend urgently need a job. Mei had given birth to Xin-Yi a day before her husband, Cho Yi, died in a fall from a scaffold and the builder refused to pay compensation, claiming Yi had ignored safety rules. Mei feared her grief would depress the job interview, but Lin had encouraged her to meet Kim, wearing her best dress and best effort at a smile.

Mei had felt at ease with Kim as soon as he greeted her; evidently Lin had explained her situation, as he was kindness personified. Some rich men she'd met as a restaurant chef were self-centered, but he was willing to adapt his life to fit her needs, and said: "We mustn't disrupt little Xin-Yi's life. All I know about babies is they need attention. Feeding and... its aftermath. But could you arrive by five every day to make and serve dinner? Is then to about nine-thirty possible?"

Mei thought of Yi's six o'clock feed and having to leave breast milk for a friend to give him, and then of her need for friends to cover working seven nights a week. She realized that her concerns must be obvious when Kim's tone became soothing.

"Bring Xin-Yi to sleep in my home while you cook. And until you settle in, I'll have Lin or Lan stay as your sous-chef-cum-nursery-aid. Does that sound all right?"

Mei thought nothing could sound better, but he topped it by offering a generous salary and referring to future benefits. She'd had to ask: "Like...could you give me an example?"

"I could do things for you... Find a home close to mine so you can spend more time with your boy, or get him in a good school. And if you ever need anything... Well, just ask."

Mei had felt surging emotions and wanted to hug Kim to express her gratitude and joy, but had enough composure to ask: "So... Do you mean I've got the job?"

"Actually, you've had it since Lin gave me your C-V and Culinary Institute diploma. But now I see my home will have a fine chef who is also a charming woman."

Since then, all had been better than Mei could have dreamed. She not only had the kitchen of her dreams, but also felt comfortable with Kim and Luan, despite odd duties caused by their quirks. Kim never hosted dinners at home; he rented a restaurant and its staff, with Mei as chef. As odd were Luan's random demands to be served her meal down in her suite, instead of dining with Kim. Mei was glad that a year before she'd begun working for Kim he replaced a spiral staircase from his penthouse to Luan's suite with an elevator.

As he had offered, Kim bought Mei an apartment just ten minutes by taxi from his home. It wasn't a gift; he set her previous rent rate for repayments, but it gave her more living space for the same amount. Mei was elated by that, and by owning a home for the first time.

Five years later, it was Kim who was elated when he could tell Mei that he'd enrolled Xin-Yi in an elite school. The joy they shared about that had led to one-too-many bottles of Pol Roger; they spent the night in his bed. The next morning's difficult conversations had eventually agreed that it was sensually pleasing, and welcome to repeat as non-committal intimacy. Both of them made every effort to sustain that agreement, but their bond of affection became increasingly evident to each other over the years.

With images of their playful sex in mind, and the clock reminding her to get going, Mei hurried to her room for clean underwear and toiletries. She came out calling: "Yi, sweetie. I'll be late, so I'll have Lin come over till your bed time. Okay?"

"I'm okay alone," he said, as he came for a kiss before rushing back to his room. It revived thoughts of Luan's lonely life, which could upset Kim at dinner. Mei stopped at the front door to think, aware that she would have to react carefully to whatever he said about his mother's life, but not knowing what he knew of it.

One heavy drinking night, Luan was remarkably open about Kim not knowing how his father had made return to Australia impossible. She had been proud of raising Kim to hate Singapore's militaristic pressures on life, from which Mei had inferred that her husband had been a soldier. Another night, Luan implied that she had to hide the Haisin's true identities.

Mei knew to avoid that unless Kim proved that he knew about that in something he said, but Luan had also let slip secrets that she deliberately kept from him. He was unaware of her storage unit of items sent from Australia, presumably by her husband in the months between their leaving and his death. Mei knew of that time-span from when a maudlin Luan had bemoaned how sudden events can have life-long effects.

She supposed that Kim's driver knew all that; Ron took Luan to her storage unit when Kim was away and stayed to drive her home. Mei wondered if she could now ask Ron, or Lin and Lan, what they knew without exposing the secrets she had, having vowed to Luan that she'd never repeat what they discussed. Nights of drinking with Luan, who talked to her as if to a ghostly image, had led to Mei researching Australian news in 1985. She had found no positive link between anything on the Internet and the Haisins, but was instinctively sure that all she'd read held the key to explaining their lives in Singapore.

1985's biggest news was the assassination of the Prime Minister, which Federal Police said 'smelled of military skills'. People labeled conspiracy theorists had pointed to resignations of Country Party conservative extremists as proof of involvement in hiring military mercenaries to remove the man responsible for socially progressive laws. Mei had sensed while researching all of this, and was now too-close-for-comfort certain, that Luan's husband was involved, somehow.

She steeled her resolve, ran out to the taxi that Kim had arranged for every day at 4:45, and apologized to the driver for being late. He smiled, glad to have the cute widow as a regular fare, but still asked: "The usual place?" He watched her nod in his mirror, smiled at her reflection as it became pensive, and drove away.

Mei sat sifting feelings about Kim, who she saw as truly loveable, and often thought what she felt must be love. However, in calmer assessment she knew it could be gratitude for his generous care. She'd tried to get Kim to express his feelings, but had either done it too subtly, or he was too astute to respond honestly. Now that Luan's death would change his life, Mei hoped she could tell him all she knew so they could build their relationship on a new level of trust. The more she tried to see what she could do to start that discussion, the more impossibly complex it seemed.

As usual, she accepted Kim as a darling friend who was most comfortable in himself when they were in bed; they had long ago agreed it was never to be a place for declaring love or scorning it. Mei tried to believe that she simply admired Kim's goodness and enjoyed his skillfully gentle love-making, but as the taxi reached his building she was hoping that, despite the day he'd endured, he could feel amorous tonight. She wanted to enjoy a diversion from dealing with difficult topics; she felt troubled enough with revived thoughts about Kim's father being paid to kill. If she allowed herself to seek the logical extension of that, it would force her to accept that Kim's wealth was launched from what must have been a massive fee for assassinating Australia's leader.

FAREWELL

She looked across the aisle into the eyes of... who? One of the business partners? She should know, she knew, but her eyes and mind were at odds today. As she returned his grim smile, he turned to listen to whoever was delivering the eulogy. She tried to do the same, but the voice sounded like it spoke some alien language.

It's... What's-his-name? He speaks English, so...

She could feel the lunchtime Valium trapping her senses in a malfunctioning mist and her feelings in an emotional void. She was aware of surreptitious glances that seemed aimed at her dried tears, and wondered if crying now would show she wasn't putting on a brave face. Maybe crying could help her to feel the sadness that must be inside. Maybe not.

Some must be my friends... they know I don't do facades.

She allowed herself a sideways glance past her son and daughter-in-law to where her daughters sat with their husbands. Seeing the girls sobbing melted her mist into flowing tears again.

Poor babies are desolate. I wish I could reach them.

Her son squeezed her hand to offer comfort, but his red eyes pleaded for her to comfort him. She couldn't encourage his belief in an afterlife that she'd rejected years ago, but put on her best motherly expression as a gesture of complicity in grief.

It's tearing them apart. They're so young, and all they know is that their Dad was too young to...

The droning eulogy begun to make vague sense, so she peered at the speaker, who looked to be in a bubble until she wiped away tears. That prompted a solemn nod from him as he went on: "...so our hearts go out to his family, who lost a devoted husband and father... a fine man we all knew. To Joseph, Samantha, Natalie..."

It's Joey, Sam and Nat! Only their Gran used those names... And me, when they exhausted my patience, like their...

Her mind filled with old resentment about how the family used male equivalents of the girls' names. She'd never known why their father insisted on calling such a pretty girl 'Sam', or named an even cuter one Natalie to be called 'Nat'. He'd ignored queries about that, along with all her suggestions for names.

I shouldn't think about it. Not here. Not now that...

A murmur alerted her to What's-his-name leaving the pulpit to an atmosphere of acclaim for the eulogy she missed. His eyes demanded praise for all the words he'd piled on the coffin in their midst, so she mouthed 'thanks' with a glance at her family to include theirs. Apparently believing his eulogy was due more than that, he returned to his pew, where he sat encouraging overt accolades from all around him.

Watching his amble up the aisle had made her aware of elusively familiar faces, all seemingly hesitant to look at her. She wondered if widows should sit at the altar to see who had cared enough to come to such numbing services, but knew that she couldn't face the congregation... especially What's-his-name, who didn't even know what everyone calls the kids.

What...is...his...name? Blank! No more Valium for me today!

She was surprised by feeling her tears flowing again, and was trying to recall what provoked them when she heard her name and tuned-in to: "...our prayers are with you now that life seems wretched, but it is really your time to rejoice. We know that he will live forever with our Lord in the kingdom above."

She let her stare at the old Pastor exude disdain for his platitudes, but his sympathetic look in response confused her until she heard her sobs and realized they were coming from her. As his rejoicing soared over the congregation's sniffles, she rested her head on Joey's shoulder and stared up at dusty roof beams in the hope that focusing on them would distract her from hearing worthless words.

They should let widows sit up there so we could really look down on preachers.

She giggled at her joke, unaware that all around heard it as crying, but had to regain her poise when the congregation rose. She'd lost count of how often they'd stood and sat, but hoped this was the last. Evidently it was; Amazing Grace was playing and the Pastor asked them to offer their fond farewells in prayers. She then saw the coffin rolling to parting curtains that she hadn't noticed before, and a tiny doorway beyond them.

It's... all over? What now? Damn. I can't tell him that I did love him... in my way... as best I could.

IN MEMORIAM

Now thinking back on it, I remember that the first time I heard of a *charn privé* was in overhearing my Scottish friend, Bruce MacDonald, mention it in one of his discourses at a party. My interest in words led me to Google the term later, but I found no listing. I either didn't search enough, or wrongly input the phonetics I heard – Autocorrect was no help. I have since learned that a *charn privé* has to be the quaintest type – and, of course, name – of a memorial monument.

Charn, pronounced like *Kahn* as in Genghis, is an old Celtic-Scot word that evolved to *cairn*, the term for piled rocks that mark borders, graves, or historic battle sites, chiefly of monumentally tragic defeats. When it's coupled with *privé*, French for private, the old Scottish term denotes a personally private memorial.

I finally heard all that on another of Bruce's trips from Scotland; he dined at my home and, as that is a too-infrequent event, we did some serious drinking. He told me that the French language was widely spoken in several periods of Scotland's history, and words often got linked to those in Scottish dialects. However, this blend, with an ancient word like *charn*, is quite rare. Bruce expanded his point by noting that French was primarily spoken by the Scottish hero, Bonnie Prince Charlie, and by Mary, of Queen of Scots fame.

I believe Bruce because, although he never brags of it, among his Edinburgh University degrees is a PhD in Scot-Celt lore. His affluent family, with its generations of academics, indulged his interest in the minutia of Scottish history. With all those geek genes, it was no surprise that Bruce traced his all-Scot ancestry back to the year dot, and that is something he does brag about after only a few drinks.

So, that night, over a bottle of Glenkinchie Single Malt from a centuries-old distillery to the south-east of Edinburgh, he rattled-off lots of that minutia. I should note that, although educated in Edinburgh and now living in Pencaitland where Glenkinchie is distilled, Bruce's almost impenetrable brogue blends numerous dialectic influences with Glasgow's guttural impact. It takes some getting used to, but I have, and all that he said was as entertaining and engrossing as always.

I had to wait a while for him to get to *charns privé*, but it was no hardship; I drank with him, unable and unwilling to interrupt. However, although I remember little of the history he recounted, I do recall that his lecture on the topic included that erecting *charns privé* could have been begun by the ancient Picts. He also said something like...

"*Dinnae think of it like it's a typical cairn, built tae be a free-standin' eye-catcher. It's nae a bit like tha', which is part o' its charm. For a start, it's no' a fucken great heap o' rocks like cairns ye see all o'er Scotland, but a wee pile o' pebbles in a discrete corner. They often used tae be in joints o' buttresses with church walls, usu'ly on the side nearest the graveyard where a lover lies, so as ye walk by ye'll see the reminder and take tha' moment tae think o' nought but the dead'un. A mind full o' images o' a lost love is lovely, don't ye think? Be'er yet, because ye ken where the wee pile is, those images start tae come tae ye as ye approach it, anticipatin' wha' ye'll see. An' what ye'll feel. No' tha' ye have tae build the fuckers anywhere near a church. Way back when folk had tae walk ev'rywhere, 'twas common tae see a charn privé where a tree's trunk and a pair o' roots form a nook tha'll protect a pile from all but scamperin' squirrels.*"

I related to all Bruce said; I was still grieving the death at just nine years old of my adopted boy, and the images in his words stuck with me long after our drink-fueled discussion. I'd seen trees with recesses between their exposed roots, because until my boy died a year earlier, we'd regularly walk the tree-lined roads of my rural community. I know he loved to scamper about in the tree-shaded areas, and I loved the idea of having a reminder of him to focus my memories whenever I was where he and I had once walked.

With that in mind, I found a tree with an indented trunk above a nook between exposed roots. It stood on an unkempt edge of a field, a serene setting to augment the *charn privé* concept. That day I started searching for suitable stones to make my boy's memorial, taking smooth, shiny-white river pebbles that would be visible at a distance.

Soon that nook held hundreds of stones, carefully stacked and looking like a cone's sector. I was pleased by my creation, and by finding that I could see a splash of white at the tree's base from fifty yards off. Just as pleasing was that even before I saw it, my mind filled with memories of my beloved little guy being there that stayed with me long after I'd passed the *charn privé*. I knew that animals could scatter the pile, or kids could deliberately destroy it, and that I'd have to deal with my special place's desecration if it happened; such is life.

That day came two weeks after I built my *charn privé*; I saw it flattened and scattered. Instead of being angry, frustrated, or the like, confronting the damage gave me insight to why the tiny memorials are special. To build one is to know why making an apparently useless pile of pebbles is worth the time and effort, and the embarrassment of being seen doing it. I saw that we build them out of the joy of having shared some of our life with another, and are lifted to make the effort by the memories that lighten the sad burden of grief.

Of course I rebuilt my *wee pile*, and still have to tidy it up sometimes, but it's no longer merely a trigger for my best memories; just to think of going for walks brings back all the lovely feelings associated with them. That helps me see what I should do to give friends and loved ones the best of me for their fond reveries. I've always tried to be kind and caring, and amusing, and seem to succeed surprisingly often, but I now try to be the best I can be, and hide dark thoughts that might be blighting the private me. I've long rejected any afterlife that religions promise, and now see the only afterlife for me will be a parallel to my unexpressed feelings for my adopted boy: *He lives while loving memories can withstand the pain of fading.*

These days, as I walk by that *charn privé* with my new adopted boy, who the rescue shelter people said is "a Havanese-Lhasa Apso mix", I delight in pausing for him to claim the tree as his own in that *privé* way of dogs. In those peacefully shared moments, I feel that my previous boy, my gone-too-early Scottish Terrier, is with us, happy to be there making our family of loving care complete.

So Lo

Detective-Specialist Lo Cunxin was alone on Police Headquarters' sixth floor at 11:30 P.M. He was reading crime scene reports of the murdered drug lord, Dmitri Karp, while trying to ignore concerns about his and his parents' lives. He succeeded enough with the latter to let him see how to benefit from what he was reading; life had taught him to be opportunistic.

His family lived over the Half Moon Café that they ran for an owner opening a classier Gold Moon Café. His two oldest brothers were villains who built a Tong-like gang; the real Tong killed them. The third idolized that pair; he hid from the Tong and wasn't seen again. The fourth worked at an airport, and got drugs past Customs for a gang he wouldn't identify; he was jailed for smuggling, and most of his parents' savings went on legal costs. A mentally unstable fifth son was the only sibling also living at home, and his medical costs took most of his parents' income. They couldn't send Cunxin to college; he was the sixth son, their lowest priority.

So, after his high school graduation, Cunxin had to work in the Half Moon Café. Police often ate there, and when he heard a few talk of being unable to understand a Chinese rape victim, he offered to interpret. That got him a job as Chinatown Precinct's clerk-translator, and his good work was rewarded by admission to the Police Academy. Graduating top of his class, he returned to his precinct thinking his career would soar, but had to wait for two years before being called downtown to see Deputy Inspector Jack Barton and Captain Jim Feeney.

At Headquarters, Barton was candid. "You make my job hard, Lo. I know you're smart, and you and your folks are clean, but your brothers were scum and you're tied to that. Got it?"

"Yes, sir. I became a Policeman to atone for my brothers shaming us. My precinct Captain can tell you I try to outsmart criminals to make Chinatown safe for everyone, and drug-free."

"And I'll use that brain to help Feeney till I can put you on cases." Barton smirked. "Practice that atoning bit, did you?"

Cunxin had replied: "I didn't know why I had to report here today, sir, so how could I?"

Now, two years later, he still reviewed stalled cases, as Feeney had first assigned. Although he found lines of inquiries for many, his career was also stalled. He let his mind drift back five hours, when he'd gone home for dinner and seen his father with Tom Wu, the Half Moon's owner. His father had looked unusually bleak, so when Wu left, he'd asked why.

"Tommy offer me Half Moon and the building."

"Wow, Pop, that's great! Does Ma know?"

"No, and not great. Price five hundred grand, but I have not even deposit. Will be hard to tell your mother we must go. But Tommy want to off-load this place."

Many thoughts collided in Cunxin's mind until he'd said: "No, Pop, I'll find a way for you, so don't tell Ma. Just tell Tom you'll need a week to get the money."

Cunxin returned to work from dinner, studied files and found clues to Dmitri Karp's hidden drug assets. Still mulling a plan to get them, he took the files home to a sub-apartment that he'd fashioned from his dead brothers' rooms, where he lay awake reading in bed.

~ ~ ~

Next day, as he arrived at Headquarters' Forensics Department, the receptionist phoned someone to say: "I think he's here." Cunxin didn't introduce himself, so was surprised, but more so by the arrival of a woman with a vivacious face and opulent figure. Her smile showed that she was used to being admired, and knew Cunxin was staring at her.

"Detective Lo Cunxin, I presume." She ended his shock with: "My log book had that name signing out files last night, and I see you've got them this morning. No mystery."

Cunxin saw her dark eyes glint and he smiled. "Ah, yes. Logic in action. Always good to see that."

"It is. But do I call you Lo, or Cunxin? Not sure for Chinese. I'm Angela Cimiletti...I run this dungeon."

"Family name is Lo. I am the sixth son, Cunxin."

"Really? So your mom called: Come here number six son?"

"Sort of. My older brother Cunfar is the fifth son. First was Cuncia, then Cunyuan, Cunmao, and fourth was Cunsang."

Her laugh jiggled deep cleavage in a low-buttoned shirt under an open laboratory coat, almost distracting him from: "That beats my logic! Forget about names, just number the kids! But do I call you Cunxin, friendly, or Lo, businesslike?"

He tried another smile. "Being friendly is good."

"Agreed! So you're Cunxin, and you call me Angie. But I need some explaining from you, so come to my office."

He trailed along, admiring her confident lope and spicy perfume, and recalling all he'd read in hopes of finding a way to work in Forensics. He knew that two senior police officers were her bosses, but two PhDs qualified Angie to direct staff scientists and medical examiners as she saw fit. He'd also seen photos of her, but they hadn't prepared him for this vibrant woman, and he felt like a boy with a crush on a teacher as he sat in her office.

To at least appear poised, he asked: "Explain what?

I've been borrowing your files for two years."

"Not coffin files." She had to explain: "Best left for dead, like unlamented drug lord, Dmitri Karp's. Upstairs think some client killed him, and did us all a good deed."

"So... no one cares about finding the killer?"

Angie shrugged. "He died in his last drug lab... no more hunting for every new one. That's it... all over for him."

Cunxin said: "But it's fascinating. Your report said the shot wasn't heard... used a silencer. Went through his wet shirt at close range... no powder burn, no bullet found. No junkie did it... they'd be frisked going in the lab. So Karp trusted the killer, who used that to wait for the right chance to shoot him. That, plus what the killer took... which is odd, plus what it seems he left there... if so, even odder... makes this fascinating, as I said."

Angie shrugged again. "No, just academic... to us. I'd say that only we two care enough to want all the facts."

Cunxin said: "But obviously someone wants Karp's supplies, so we should let upstairs know that a drug ring is expanding. We won't know whose if we stop now."

She frowned. "Crime scene tapes come down this week, and if nobody cares, and other work is burying us, why go on?"

"Or... Why not try to stop an unknown drug ring? I'd rather investigate it than read reports." He grinned. "Even yours"

"Flattery so I'll let you go play there, kiddo?" She covered her allusion to their decade age difference with: "If our top case reviewer says to not shelve this, who am I to say no to him?"

"So we can go there now?"

"No-no! I have real work to do before we play. Be here at one and I'll take you to the 'fascinating' dump."

~ ~ ~

At lunchtime, Angie led Cunxin to a Jeep littered

with laboratory equipment. He wondered how a smart woman could be so untidy, and why he felt so happy to be with her, but knew that both answers lay in Angie's infectious exuberance for life.

After they put on gloves and lab coats at Karp's cramped lab, Angie waited just inside the bullet-proof door while Cunxin inspected the room. He gestured for her to stay where she was, then said: "So, the killer's mistakes left us some clues."

"And you see that...where?"

"Too many boxes of latex glove for drug handling. They're packaging. In those wire loops on that tray go gloves, tops open to get a hundred milligrams of dope. Taped up and back in hundred gloves boxes, now a kilo of ten, labelled 'medical supplies'. But these..." From a shelf of glove boxes in ten rows piled five high and two deep, Cunxin took a pile and said: "Unopened, ditto, ditto, ditto...and this." He threw a box to her. "Take it to the window's light. Carefully! Don't stir up dust."

As she headed away, he moved ten sealed gloves from a box he'd said was unopened into his lab coat pockets before she turned back, holding up ten similar gloves. "I looked in a box or two, saw gloves, so I missed these! I see now it'd take years for the few people who'd fit in here to use all these gloves."

Cunxin held up the box he had just emptied. "Karp put empties back to keep stacks even. Seeing missing boxes could tempt people to open some, but with neat stacks they'd see no reason to wonder about them."

Angie stared at the shelf, slowly nodding approval of his theory, but said only: "So, a Psychology major?"

He ignored that and went on with: "To the bullet... Your report noted that the killer had to be at the sink for the shot to enter at close range, hit his heart and nick rib six to exit. A direct line from the sink hits the wall behind him, but his body fell a bit to one side... it's in the scene photos, so he had to be turning as the killer fired. See the dust on the little table to your left? Any thoughts about the square and circle shapes in it?"

She shrugged. "That the killer took whatever it was that made that square... right? The circle was a jug."

"Yes, and the glass on the floor came from it."

"So evidently Karp bumped a water jug as he fell... what of it?"

"I thought from the photo that glass held clues. Now I'm sure." Seeing her evaluating that, he relaxed his lecturing tone and pointed to the glass. "On top of shards from the fall is powdery glass. I'd say from a bullet's impact after it bounced off the scales that made the square shape in the table's dust."

She assessed a trajectory via Karp to the square, jug and a wall at right angles to where she had expected. Behind items the police search had moved to that wall, she dug out a bullet from a small hole in the base board. "Mangled, but could match the small entry wound in Karp. My lab will confirm it. So... what now?"

"If I proved it is worth more sleuthing, we can go, but I'd like to come back tomorrow and check it all."

Angie laughed. "Well, okay, I'll let you play here... if you tell me how to explain the lack of powder burns, and only water on Karp's chest."

"The killer's at the sink... fills a glove with water and fires through it. It muffles the shot, and water traps the gunpowder. Now, the killer, or his boss, is after Karp's drugs. But he took only the scales... maybe his bullet's ricochet left some distinctive mark your team could identify. Will that explain it for you?"

"Should... and you were right. It is fascinating!"

On the drive back, Angie asked why the killer didn't take the drugs. Cunxin suggested that he couldn't find them, then asked why the police or her team didn't find any or the bullet. She said no one cared that Karp was killed, so no one made much of an effort, and thanked him for the reminder to not do that. Cunxin smiled enigmatically, now seeing real hope for his career, and for buying the Half Moon Café for his parents.

~ ~ ~

Next morning Cunxin was alone at Karp's lab, finding every box of drugs and weighing its gloves on scales borrowed from his mother. A box of ten held a $100,000 street value kilogram of heroin, and he had $900,000 worth piled up, plus $100,000 at home, with only Angie knowing any of it was there. To be sure he hadn't missed anything, he rechecked and saw a box marked by a tiny ink dot, as were the drug-filled gloves inside it. Cunxin deduced that dot-marked gloves and boxes held pure heroin that would almost double the total worth of the drugs.

He put the ten ink-dotted gloves, forty of drugs cut with powdered milk, and the scales in his bag. Before restacking the boxes, Cunxin put ink dots on the four boxes of drug-filled gloves that he would leave so he could say it was how Karp identified which held drugs. After taking photos to support this fiction, he left.

At the Half Moon Café, he ran through the kitchen, where his parents and staff were preparing for a lunch rush, pointing to being dusty as he went by his mother. In his rooms, he hid the drugs in a sleeper-sofa with the prior day's haul, took another jacket, and went back down. When his mother stopped him to fix its collar, as if needing to fuss over her one good son, Cunxin invited her to see Cunsang in jail; he knew she couldn't go.

"Not now, Cunxin! Lunch. Go later see Cunsang?"

"Sorry, Ma. I've got to work later. It's now or not."

Mrs. Lo grunted her anguish, and mumbled sadly: "You tell Cunsang...tell I miss him."

"He knows." After gently kissing her brow, he said: "But I'll tell him...and say that you still love him. Bye."

At the prison, his Detectives' Shield got him to the Duty Officer. A plausibly told story of needing to see his brother as part of an undercover drugs investigation got full cooperation. Cunxin was taken to a room where Cunsang was already sitting, handcuffed to a chair and suspiciously eyeing the room.

Cunxin told him: "Not bugged. Can't chat, but Ma sends her love." When Cunsang smiled, he said: "That gang you can't discuss... Can you get them a message?" Cunsang considered the implications in that before he nodded. "Good. So let's talk about a way to help Pop that will help you. I have a kilo of pure heroin and five of street dope that I'll sell for half a million so Pop can buy the Half Moon and the whole building."

Cunsang said that the price was too low, and was worried when he heard that Cunxin had assumed a kilo was pure; he'd seen men killed for misrepresenting drugs. When that didn't alarm his brother, Cunsang returned to the topic of telling the gang about the drugs for sale, and got Cunxin's attention with: "One's here... We talk. He'll tell the others if this sounds okay."

Cunxin smiled. "It will." He then asked seriously: "But do they have the money?"

His brother smirked. "Shit yeah! The gang bosses, the McGrath brothers, have a coke-head stock broker cousin. He 'invests' in drug deals with black cash he gets from clients for insider trading tips." Cunsang went on to explain how to give test samples and swap drugs for cash, and ended with how he would avoid exposing his brother. "I'll say it's Tong dope... Nobody fucks with them. But how does any of this help me?"

"I can get Headquarters to support paroling you for your help, and Ma and Pop will hire this parolee in their restaurant."

Back at work, Cunxin phoned Feeney to report that the media could be told of drugs found in Karp's lab, but without naming him, as his brother feared revenge for informing. After the call, he expanded on all he had told Angie in a detailed report that had photos of drugs in gloves, ink-dotted boxes, and stacked boxes. After emailing it to Angie, with copies to her bosses, and Feeney and Barton, he left work feeling drained.

~ ~ ~

Next day, a highly gratifying email was on his office computer:

Thank you for an excellent report, Detective Lo. It makes a valid case for continuing the investigation of Karp's killer, if he was hired and by whom, to find where that drug supply will go. I look forward to working with you on this and other cases - you have an exceptional ability to analyze data and deduce perfectly reasonable hypotheses for investigation.

Dr. Angela F. Cimiletti, Forensics Division Director

As copies went to all he had copied on his report, when Feeney's secretary phoned to summon him up, Cunxin assumed his boss would also compliment him. He was unprepared for the greeting he got.

"Listen, Lo! My... eyes at the Pen said you saw your drug runner brother. Your report says Karp got killed for his drugs... what's the connection? I know you lied about being undercover to see him, but me and Barton stuck our necks out for you, given your family's record, so you need to explain this right now!"

Cunxin looked contrite. "Sorry, I should have said up-front. I figured he could find out who wants Karp's gear. We aren't close... he's like our big brothers, but I'm the only cop he'd talk to, so I made him an offer... If he points us the right way, I'd keep his name out of it and try to get him paroled. That okay?"

Feeney nodded, but was stern. "Be sure he doesn't feed us bullshit! And that doesn't explain why you lied to see him."

Showing surprise that his boss didn't see it, Cunxin said: "I couldn't talk out there about the drugs at Karp's lab. Other than Angie... Miz Cimiletti... you had to be the first to know."

Feeney's face showed approval, but his tone stayed gruff. "So you remember to keep me in the loop on everything! Now beat it."

At his desk, Cunxin wrote sequenced reminders of parts of his plan on Post It Notes, all in Chinese. He then phoned Tom Wu, asked to meet him that night, and said he'd like to dine at the Gold Moon. The phone rang just after he hung up.

"It's Angie. Listen. I let upstairs know that if they failed and my bosses chintzed on checking out Karp's murder, we're lucky to have you. You're Golden Boy, and I'm glad. In case I didn't say it, you're a treat to work with after the usual idiots on my cases, so I'll buy you a drink tonight to toast our teamwork."

"Love to, but I'm going to a Chinatown restaurant. We could drink there... or have dinner, if you're free. But I'll have to leave you for a little while for a meeting. That be okay?"

"Not okay, fabulous! I heard eating with Chinese gets Chinatown's best food, so... yes! Absolutely yes!"

Cunxin told her the address to meet him at seven, then packed what he needed to create faux agreements at home for the Half Moon's sale so nothing was on his office computer. He left a note that he was investigating the Karp case, took his Post It reminders, and slipped out of the office.

~ ~ ~

He reached the restaurant before seven and told Wu of a friend coming for dinner to explain having to delay their meeting until after that. Wu was asking why they had to meet at all when Angie made an entrance; along with a dazzling smile she wore a bright red, side-slit, tight cheongsam dress that showcased her figure.

"Appropriate?" She asked Cunxin. "New place, and you know the owner! Oh, this will be lovely... Let's eat!"

Wu slid in to introduce himself and compliment Angie's dress for a Chinatown visit, then led them to a table. As Cunxin and Angie chatted over dinner and wine, he kept alert and saw Wu take cigarettes out to the parking lot. After apologetically reminding Angie of his meeting, he hurried outside.

He began: "Mister Wu, about Dad's money, you–"

"I won't hold a mortgage!" Wu snapped, but then softened his tone. "Your father said he needs a week. Do you promise that?"

"Yes, but I'm getting the cash from guys who hate cops and don't know I'm one. So I need you to be my go-between. Don't worry... they're not the Tong."

Wu smiled. "Tong men do not worry me."

Cunxin explained his need for help with messages and a meeting. Wu guessed it would be a drug deal and joked it would be Chinese Street Theater by bad guys. Cunxin smiled thinly as he gave Wu a sealed envelope of pure and cut heroin samples, along with instructions for proceeding. "A man will get it tomorrow. Thanks for helping, Mister Wu, but I must go in to Angie."

Wu smiled, slyly. "How does a boy like you get a hot mama like that, Baby Lo?"

Cunxin said: "We're just friends from work."

Both returned inside and saw Angie checking her watch, eager to leave. Wu waved-off a waiter bringing their check, and savored Angie's effusive thanks. Out at their cars, she kissed Cunxin's cheek before driving off, which eased his concerns, but with seemingly endless preparations to do, he hurried home.

~ ~ ~

Cunxin hoped his shower next morning revived him for a hard day after getting no sleep. His first task was to convince his father to accept and sign papers.

"Date wrong, Cunxin! This say five year ago!"

"On paper, it's when you got the mortgage. The next says Tom held it, interest-free if you paid in five years." To ease his father's concern, Cunxin said: "Tom agreed to this, so just sign. He'll sign the one that you paid in full, after he gets the money."

"But Cunxin... I have no money for Tommy!"

"You just don't know where it is, Pop, and that's a good thing."

Pop Lo signed the papers, sadly suspicious that his last son might also be a criminal, but fearing loss of his home and job at his age if he didn't. Cunxin smiled to reassure his father before gathering up the papers and hurrying to Police Headquarters.

At work, he phoned Captain Feeney's office for a meeting and was told to come up. After checking his Post It reminders of what he needed from the meeting, he ran upstairs to find his boss was waiting at the door.

"Make it fast, Lo. I've got people coming soon."

"Thanks for not naming me at the media brief on Karp's half million bucks of dope. But I'm here about my brother. He won't talk in jail... you're not the only one with eyes there. I can get him to fake an illness to go to hospital so we can talk, and have the jail call you to confirm I can take him. Will you do it?"

"Asking a fucking lot, Lo! Why should I stick my neck out calling in a lot of favors to help you do that?'

"If I've figured right, sir, you'll nab the gang my brother worked for, get all their drugs, and their money man's name."

Captain Feeney's elation surfaced. "O-fucking-kay! Go do it, Lo. For that result...yeah, I'll back you up."

The jail's Duty Officer told Cunxin that Feeney called to set up a permit for him to meet his brother in a hall for trustees. He found Cunsang there, and after a scan of the room to see if officers seemed interested in them, he said: "Pop's afraid your bad gall bladder and pancreatitis will give you spasms in here. He said you get gut-wrenching pains across the middle, under your ribs. I didn't know that. Are you okay?"

Cunsang showed he would follow his brother's lead with: "No, but I can't show it. Any weakness in here is... You know."

Cunxin poked his own chest. "Pop said you can't lie, sit, or stand to ease the pain, and you don't have your meds. Why?"

Now sure Cunxin knew about the illness, Cunsang said: "In here, meds that don't get you high are seen as a weakness! But I can feel it coming on now, and... like, all that pain is starting."

Cunxin prompted: "Can't swallow or burp to clear it, and it's hard to breathe? Must be hell! Should you go to hospital?"

Cunsang jolted up to a stooped stance, clutched his chest and gasped: "I should. Will they let me go?"

Cunxin ran to a guard, calling back: "I'll see to it! But stay as still as you can...breathe slowly. It'll help."

In an ambulance that Feeney expedited, Cunxin told Cunsang in Chinese how to fake his illness, and in return heard the gang member's names and where they hid drugs. As they got near the hospital, Cunsang told the driver's assistant that his pains were easing, and that was conveyed ahead by radio.

By the time a doctor examined Cunsang, he knew to ask for Hyoscyamine pills for under his tongue if his pain returned. Cunxin slipped away to phone Feeney to say he'd learned some important gang facts, and to ask for an officer to bring him a car, take his brother back to jail in an ambulance and bring his car from there to Headquarters. He knew Feeney wanted the publicity of a major arrest, so expected a cop and car soon.

When that car arrived, Cunxin drove to work via a stop at a 7-11 to call Wu to make sure the envelope was taken and all else arranged. At his office, glad that the 7-11 phone avoided a record of his call, he reviewed his Post It Notes and saw he'd have to handle one aspect in person, so he called Wu and said: "Can't talk. I'm at work, but I had to tell you I'll be at the Street Theater." He hung-up as a call came in from Captain Feeney.

"Sir, I was just about to call and ask if I can come up and fill you in on... Now? Okay, on my way."

Feeney greeted him with: "Shit, Lo, you look all in!"

He flopped on a chair. "Just need sleep, sir. Now, I don't have it all, and if the rumors are wrong it'll be a wild goose chase... and you'll have to hide the Lo name to keep my brother safe... Without Cunsang, no—"

Feeney snapped: "I get it! I didn't get this rank without some fuck-ups and secrets, so just tell me what this is and how it goes from here... wild geese and all."

Cunxin said: "Chinatown and jail rumors say the Tong's selling heroin tomorrow night to the gang my brother knew—"

"Where'd you get that info?" Feeney interjected.

"No! My family's at risk. I can tell you I'll hear when the deal will be done... probably near that self-storage place outside Chinatown. You need hidden cars ready to go when I call you."

Feeney said warily: "You want teams waiting to be told where the drug gang is? Do we get Tong guys, too?"

Cunxin quashed a laugh. "In Chinatown? They'll vanish, and you won't know in time to hit the meeting. But you can grab the gang and the drugs after it."

Feeney stared at his Detective. "You're my team's brains, Lo, so if you pull this off and we get the gang, the dope and... You mentioned a money man?"

'Some high-flying, coke-snorting stock broker."

Feeney laughed. "I love nabbing them! Their faces

as it sinks in that they'll do time... priceless! But, as I was saying... if this goes well, it'll be hard to keep you. There's a push to move you that I can't talk about, but I'll be fighting it."

Appearing to be glad of that, Cunxin said: "Thanks. But back to the squad cars... Hide them on the storage place side of Chinatown. I'll hear the deal's going down and get close to it... my face fits in, and phone your cell with the way the cars leave. Okay?"

"Yeah, it's good, Lo. Real good. Now go home and get some sleep so you can do all you have to for me."

Cunxin had to leave via his office, as he had to call Angie. When she answered, he said: "Someone wants your golden boy in a new job, so could you find out who, where and why?"

"Detective Lo detected it already! Jack told me."

"Deputy Inspector Barton? What did he say?"

"That you're working on something that'll make you Super Golden Boy. So... how do you like the idea of a transfer?"

"Honestly? For the last few years all I've wanted is to get into your department. But I'm not supposed to know about this, so if you hear more, can you keep me posted...privately?"

She laughed. "At the Gold Moon Café? Hang on... It's call-wait and I have to take it... Jack again. Bye."

He drove home feeling oddly jealous about Angie's rapport with Barton; it was an emotion he had always been too self-contained to allow. Tom Wu broke into his thoughts by calling his cell to say only 'Come to the Gold Moon' before hanging up.

Unlike the curt call, Wu greeted him warmly, and said: "Cells are easy to hack, and I don't want anyone hearing about your envelope collector bringing it back much lighter. Here."

Taking the envelope, Cunxin asked: "He said...?"

"That he'll be here tomorrow night...I doubt to eat. But he asked if I'm 'the' Tommy Wu, so he must know who I am."

"You're well known in Chinatown, Mister Wu. At the Half Moon, and now in this Gold Moon."

Wu grinned. "You think he knows of me because he is a fan of Chinese cuisine? Well, maybe. But what's this about you at the Street Theater? Just observing?"

"No, I want to be the one swapping my bag for one of cash, but I'm nervous about it."

Wu patted Cunxin's cheek. "No stage fright, Baby Lo. A chorus line of 'respectful' friends will be there to stop any booing."

He now knew he'd have Tong protection, but also that they could take the drugs and cash. As Wu seemed amused by his concern, Cunxin asked: "If you know how these go, Mister Wu... Will this go how I want?"

"Exactly how... if you leave no traces. Clean all you touch. Wear gloves, and a hoody, jeans and sneakers to blend in."

Cunxin tore open the envelope, glanced at a note in it and said: "They're going to be here tomorrow night at nine-thirty."

Wu frowned and led the way through the kitchen to the parking lot before saying: "Too early. Customers still in and out... We can't change it. Friends will show our visitors where to go." He pointed to a back fence's lamps. "I'll kill lights in that corner. Customers don't park where it'll be dark when they leave. We'll move any who try to, so relax, Baby Lo... Go home and sleep."

"But I have the sale papers to go over with you."

"I'll sign them and give them back with your deed. This is partly yours, right?"

Cunxin scowled. "All Pop's. I'm not involved in it."

After looking dubious, Wu grinned. "But you'll be promoted after the cops grab the buyers! Ha! Where will it be?"

Cunxin laughed. "Out near the storage center."

"Perfect! No links to my Gold Moon or you, except the guys your cops are going to try to arrest."

"Try to?"

Wu shrugged. "It's ten blocks away... Who knows? So let's hope that works for you. The rest will. Now go."

Cunxin left feeling troubled. The doubt Wu raised about arresting the gang at the storage center, where he told Feeney to go, was a problem; they could have a new stash site since his brother was jailed. Worse, with the police being so far off, if the gang headed away from the trap after the deal they might escape before squad cars could catch up. He foresaw a wild goose chase that Feeney would surely blame on him.

~ ~ ~

Despite his fatigue, Cunxin was dressed before his alarm clock went off, and went down to the restaurant's fridge. As he ate he wrapped his Post It reminders in a paper towel, then burned it in a frying pan. Wearing kitchen gloves to clean his fingerprints from the drug-filled gloves, he put them in a trash bag and cleaned it.

With drugs, jeans and sneakers in his car, Cunxin drove to work and tried to look busy. At lunchtime, he bought a hoody with an English Soccer team's logo on it to distance him from the jacket after he cast it off. As importantly, its pockets could hide his Police issue .357 Glock and a small Beretta he'd taken from a drunk in Chinatown. As the day wore on, he cleared his office of all notes about his drug deal, before emailing Captain Feeney that he would be out of touch until he phoned to confirm or call off the trap.

Feeling as ready as he ever would, he drove to the Gold Moon to wait with Tom Wu, who was alarmed by his weariness and sent him to relax on a couch in the office. Cunxin couldn't rest; behind a display of antique assaying scales from gold-rushes he saw a new set with a distinctive dent in its square base. He was too logical to see it as proof that the scales were Dmitri Karp's, or that Wu shot Karp, but the possibilities nagged at him. He lay on the couch, uncertain of how to interpret the scale's presence, and Wu's apparent ties to the Tong, who killed three of his brothers. He was considering that as he heard Wu quietly open the door, so he said without turning: "I'm awake. Did you want me?"

"You should see the set up before it gets dark."

"Yeah, sure. Just have to get my shoes back on."

Wu scowled. "No sneakers to fit in, as I told you?"

"With jeans and a hoody in my car. Do I need more?"

"Need? I hope not, but... maybe a gun... In case."

Cunxin was ready to say: "My Glock is police issue, so if I fire it I have to say I did and forensics will check it. Do you have one I can carry?"

After a pensive pause, Wu said: "Just a twenty-five cal Titan. It's a toy next to a Glock, but very good at close range. It's in my desk drawer. I'll get it."

"After I see the set up. Need the daylight, right?"

Out in the parking lot, Cunxin saw an Audi S6 at the back fence with three men in it, but only the Chinese driver's face visible. Wu pointed out the area to be ringed by 'our friends' and lights that had been removed, before saying: "Men in the car will see no one parks there. After dark, more will come to control the area and guide our visitors. You'll be in that Audi and get out like you own it." He grinned. "Feel free to swagger."

To camouflage his fear of Tong members who might know he is a Detective, Cunxin asked warily: "Shouldn't I be alone in it if I own it?."

"No, they'll expect to see a guardian. As my friend, you'll be kept safe, but show no fear of our visitors. Do we know names?"

"Hearsay... two McGrath brothers, a Riley and—"

Wu interjected: "Those Irish misfits! They drive ugly Cadillac Escalades... we'll spot them a mile off!"

Any security Cunxin felt from having expert help was offset by anxiety about Wu's familiarity with that gang and the Tong. He had to ignore it, and the scales, and if Wu shot Karp with the gun he was offered. He nodded and tried to look calm; each took an effort as he tried to keep control of the plan in his mind. He went to his car and put on his driving gloves before grabbing his clothes and bag of drugs. As Wu was still where they stood to talk, Cunxin had to speak louder than he liked. "I'll change in the office and get the... item in your desk. Which drawer? I should handle it... just in case."

Wu frowned, but seemed to dismiss a concern and said: "Top right, under a ledger... No, I should get it."

"Customers are arriving... see to them. And stay visible during our Street Theater so a room of people can say you were there, showing no sign of knowing a thing about... anything." Cunxin forced a smile. "I'll see you later, with Pop's money."

Wu winked. "You have talent, Baby Lo. See you at nine."

In Wu's office, Cunxin put down his bundles and went to get the Titan semi-automatic. He would have ignored the book on if it hadn't opened as he pulled it out, showing notes in Chinese for names in English. He stifled his curiosity and added the silver-gray gun to his couch pile, but returned to the book. He'd seen familiar names, including 'Karp', and now saw that some notes beside them in Chinese had, in English, 'X x 25'. He was glad he had handled the .25 caliber gun in gloves.

For the first time since he planned to sell the drugs he'd deduced were still at Karp's lab, Cunxin felt the conflict of his duties to the police and to his father. He eventually shrugged and, after checking that Wu was busy, returned and photocopied the ledger book. With the prints rolled in his work clothes and put in a trash bag, he tucked his Beretta in a sock, the Glock in a hoody pocket, and Wu's Titan in his belt. He didn't relax until he'd taken a cell phone photo of the dented scales, though he didn't know how he could use it.

A loud knock on the door at nine heralded a note sliding under it; it was 'NOW!' in a smiley face sketch, token cheeriness that boosted his resolve and energy. With the hood on his head and gloves on, he took his bags of clothes and drugs through the kitchen to put one bag in his car. As he took the drugs to the Audi, he saw six Chinese men in similar clothes to his, and all nodded respectfully. As surprising was the Audi driver getting out like a chauffeur to open a door. Cunxin just nodded; he'd realized that he should disguise his voice and chuckled at an idea of copying a regular Half Moon customer's Chinese accent that had amused him.

His mirth drew from the driver: "Wha' funny?"

Cunxin's shock at hearing English, not Mandarin, was replaced by gratitude for a chance to try Chinese accented English. "Jus' us. We si' an' wait. Bu' wha' for? To do deal wi' dumb Irish. Ha! All bullshit."

The driver laughed. "Fucken funny bullshi'! Plan great! We get all... Irish fuckers get all-fuck-up. Ha!"

"Ha-ha," Cunxin said flatly, as he realized the Tong had their own plan and he had only Wu's assurance of his going as he wanted. He didn't like ideas that came to him about possible Tong actions, but knew he had to go with whatever happened. In hope of doing more than that, he tested if his Tong driver would obey him. "No talk till Irish here. I sit back out o' sight till you say safe to get out. You be my eyes. You go' that?"

The man nodded and began a constant scan from the lit area to their gloomy corner. A tense Cunxin saw Tong men fade into shadows as others went towards the entrance. Soon two Escalades followed them back and stopped in their dark area, the first just three feet away. Cunxin saw Tong men wave from by the second SUV, prompting his driver to say: "Can get ou' now. I open door an' follow to guard you."

Cunxin said: "Hold gun in pocket so they see gun in it."

The driver chuckled. "Too many gun pockets for hands."

When Cunxin got out, his driver paused to let him lead, but Cunxin saw no movement from the Cadillacs, and snapped: "Tell men to show guns so just Irish see, then go back to shadows."

The message in Mandarin was instantly obeyed; as quickly, a man stepped out of each Escalade. The closer one said in an faded Irish brogue: "Put up them guns! We're wantin' no fuck ups here. Who do I talk to?"

"Me," Cunxin said, and harshly added: "Who you, an' where bag o' cash? I go' your bag, where mine?" He made his soft voice menacing. "You don' wan' me nod to my men. No. Las' thing you want...or ever see."

"Ease it up, Chinaman! Don't go threatin' me!"

"No threat. I nod, none of you leave alive. Got it?"

The second Irish-looking man came to say: "What's up, Kevin? And why are the Chinks spooked?"

Cunxin snarled: "Kevin fool! Should be easy. You bring cash, we bring all you want. Kevin go' no bag."

"Get it, Kevin! We don't fuck with spooked gooks."

As a Tong man trailed Kevin to his SUV, Cunxin asked: "Who you?"

"Tim McGrath. Can't see your face. Who are you?"

"Face no matter... call me Mao. Wha' matters is we know you an' Kevin got money!" Cunxin lowered his voice so only Tim heard. "Time to show good faith, Tim. How many guns on you? Two, I'd say... one a back-up piece. Give it to me and I'll give you mine, so we can do our deal and part amicably."

The change of tone and diction surprised Tim as much as the offer, but both seemingly convinced him that 'Mao' was not just a Tong thug. He told Kevin to hurry, and adopted a similarly civil tone. "I don't want no trouble, but I'll not pull out a gun with trigger-happy guys watching."

Cunxin told the men in Chinese to let the visitor get out a handgun. By then, Kevin had a valise there, and Cunxin told him: "Pu' down, open an' go stan' by car. I deal wi' Tim." To Tim he said: "I'm glad your brother can be trained. Now... Before you give me your piece and get mine, tell your men to stay cool... very cool."

Tim had Kevin give their men the message, and Cunxin tried to look nonchalant as he stood by the open valise to see a half-million dollars. He pulled Wu's Titan from his belt, held it flat on his gloved hand, and said: "I like this, but I'll give it up as a token of trust for future deals. On one condition... Tell me the case holds a half million in genuine bills. But first, tell me you know what'll happen to you if not. Well, Tim?"

"Yep, I packed it. Kevin always want to come out on top in deals. Not me. You and I'll be cool, Mao."

"So it's gun giving time." Cunxin put a surprisingly light Ruger .22 caliber magnum revolver in a pocket and lifted the bag of heroin. "Listen, Tim. The dope's in gloves, ten to a kilo, but the ten with an ink dot on the sealing tape are the pure stuff. Now, take this, I'll take the cash, and we'll split. Travel safely."

Cunxin took the valise into the Audi as the driver stayed poised to use his pocketed arsenal. He saw the Irish brothers swap Escalades, so Kevin left first. Only when both SUVs went towards the self-storage center did Cunxin feel he could relax, but then he remembered he had much to do.

First was to be driven to the Gold Moon's kitchen door, where he ran from the Audi to Wu's office and put the case of cash behind the couch. He was looking for Wu when he heard cacophonous gunfire nearby, so ran back through the kitchen and saw the Audi still there, the driver on a phone. In seconds he'd realized that the call was to Tong members who fired the shots. Seconds later he heard that the McGrath gang was dead and the Tong had the drugs. Cunxin pretended to be delighted.

Aware that he had to phone Feeney, he went into a dark area to call. "It's Lo, Captain... just listen! They went your way and I was about to call when I heard lots of shots. I tried to get a fix on it before calling, but it seems the gang got ambushed on the Chinatown side of the storage center. That's all I can tell you. Okay?"

"Not o-fucking-kay at all! We're at that bloodbath! Lot of bodies... but no drugs! Can you get here?"

"It'll take a while... I'm on foot, but I must tell that I heard the McGraths shot Dmitri Karp, so send every gun to Miz Cimiletti. She may solve that case for you. I'll start walking over there now."

After a snort of exasperation, Feeney said: "No, fuck it... we're here. I'll try to talk to you tomorrow."

"Oh, thanks, sir. I do need some sleep. Good night."

Cunxin was surprised by his boss' vague mention of talking instead of an order to see him tomorrow. He was also still stunned by all that had happened, but did not let any of that limit his smile as he went back inside and saw Tom Wu heading for him. He said: "I put your money in your office."

"Thanks, Baby Lo. So is your father's paperwork."

In the office, Cunxin said nothing about gunfire as Wu got out Champagne. He didn't know if that was to toast the Half Moon or the drug deal, but knew which he could discuss. "I'm not being rude, but you should celebrate with Pop. Buying the Half Moon is the best thing he and Ma have done since they left their old life in Qingdao. Plus, I need to get home... I'm so beat!"

"I see that, Baby Lo, so take the papers and deed. But I must say... I don't know what to make of you. You have a flair for tonight's business, and seem unfazed by all of it. But what do you think of all that... after? Or even know about it?"

Cunxin chose to say: "I don't want to know more than I'll hear at work. My boss is mad that he missed a gang arrest, but for me tonight, I had a purpose... get money for Pop to pay you so he and Ma can work and live in the only place they've owned, with no mortgage burden. And only I could do that for them."

Wu looked like he would say something, but just nodded and escorted Cunxin to his car, all the while praising him. As if an afterthought, Wu politely asked: "Where's my gun? In the drawer?"

Cunxin turned to face Wu, aware that he couldn't ignore all that happened. "I want you to listen, not speak. Your gun is gone. I gave it to Tim McGrath so Police would get it when they arrest him. I think the gun killed Dmitri Karp... you've heard of him. I wanted a guy who's going to jail to be blamed for Karp's murder. I'm a cop... it solves that case. But it's win-win. All he could say was that a Chink swapped it for his gun, so no link to me or you. What I'm saying is, you lost a gun, but are in the clear. You can have McGrath's Ruger, but it'll have a history, so I don't advise you get caught with it. Now, leaving that for you to ponder, I'll say goodnight and thanks again, Mister Wu."

He got to his room by eleven, feeling famished from not having eaten since breakfast. He could ignore that because a worse feeling was dismay about losing control of his plan. As a policeman, he'd seen mass killings when gang rivalries became turf wars, but none had prepared him for tonight. He also wasn't prepared for meeting a notorious criminal and liking him, so now felt guilty about setting him up for an arrest that was made worse by the intervening massacre. Cunxin had to hope that everything would look better in the morning as he fell onto his bed, and almost instantly into a deep sleep.

~ ~ ~

As he wearily entered the Half Moon's kitchen at seven, Cunxin found neighbors noisily discussing the TV news. He got through to his parents and hugged them to say: "You've bought The Half Moon! It's yours! Congratulations!" He saw their joy was marred by the TV, but his mother's smile began to glow. His father remained furious about criminals' drug wars and Irish gangsters getting shot in Chinatown.

Cunxin chose to ignore TV reports about the notorious McGrath gang and left to get ready for work. He paused to grab food his mother had put out for the neighbors as the restaurant phone rang, so answered it.

"Cunxin? Is that you?"

"Angie? Yes... what a surprise. Why are you calling here? And at this god-awful hour?"

"To tell you to get in here A-S-A-P!"

"You're at work? It's not even seven-thirty!"

"Came in at midnight. I can't talk now, so please hurry straight to my office. See you soon... Bye."

He dressed and left, trying to guess why he was so urgently needed when, as far Headquarters knew, his role was as a case analyst on undercover work. As his ideas went from ridiculous to impossible, he focused on getting to Angie to hear the facts.

The Forensic Laboratory receptionist had seen him entering and made a quick phone call, then said: "I told Angela you're here. She'll be out in a few minutes. Take a seat."

"Know why she wants to see me? The gang thing?"

The woman shrugged, so he sat near a TV showing text without sound to see the Chinatown news. He read the details until he saw Angie beckon from the hall to her office. As he got to her door, Cunxin asked: "Why'd

I have to come here?"

"Lots to do. But first, where did you go yesterday? And for what? Your cell phone was off... still is."

He couldn't see a Chinatown connection, so let her lead him to it. "I left about three to go undercover and get facts for Feeney about a drug deal that led to last night's Chinatown shit fight, so my cell was off. Why... is this connected to any of that?"

Angie chuckled. "Not exactly. But it explains why you didn't see Jack Barton's email that went out at four. He's promoted you to Detective-Specialist First Class, transferred here, as of today. I wanted you in early to talk before the Chinatown 'shit fight' has me too busy to think. Oh, there's one more thing. I'm your new boss. Is that okay with you, Cunxin?"

"To quote my new boss... Not okay, it's fabulous! I'm just going to love being here, with you."

Getting There

If you've written fiction you might relate to this, and at its end nod knowingly, thinking something along the lines of: *Yeah, I get how that works and I'm happy for you.* Well, okay...I do foresee some of you writers being inclined to mutter: *Lucky bastard! I need inspiration like that!* But this isn't really for any of you who do, or try to write fiction.

It's for you who never entered a world of endlessly creating characters and dropping them into situations where they must react to other flimsily existing people. I suppose that in your best sagacious tone, you can quote some author saying '*characters write themselves*', and exude certainty that you fully appreciate the nuances of creativity evolving with no authorial guiding hand. But let's be honest... that notion is really a mystery to you, so if you read to the end of this, your reaction will likely be: *He got an idea for ending his new novel... so what?* Or, if your mind is mathematically or engineeringly bent, I can almost hear you vehemently scoff: *No one can start a novel without knowing how it ends and having a plan for all the stuff in the middle! Not possible!*

I almost envy you. How delightful it must be to not be always writing in your mind, to not feel it echoing with loud snippets of dialogue between yet-to-flesh-out people while at check-outs or in traffic. You are blissfully ignorant of how it feels to have lots of *BITS* in your head. Start *BITS* for which you can't find a remotely plausible ending. End *BITS* that keep you awake, trying to create a story arc to that end, all the while knowing it's one of those *you can't get there from here* things. Plus *BITS* of everything you have ever seen, heard, felt or thought that can bring your fiction to life. Real life.

Such ignorance must be bliss. But for non-writers of fiction, and even non-fiction writers, I offer a sample of the creative calisthenics of my literary hero: Joseph Heller. All writers should read his *Portrait of an Artist as an Old Man*. Its protagonist is an old writer seeking inspiration for a new book's plot in a variety of opening sentences. One he tries is: "The kid, they say, was born in a manger, but, frankly, I have my doubts."

Joe used that line in a 1974 Playboy interview for the release of *Something Happened* to explain the long interval since *Catch 22*. He blamed his technique; he said he never put a word on paper until he'd mentally traced the tale from a first sentence to a last sentence that he already had. Joe said he dropped that opening sentence above because he didn't think anyone could be interested in some kid in a manger, whatever that is.

Sure, he was being wryly funny Joseph Heller, but he'd kept that gag *BIT* in his head from 1974 until he used it in what became his posthumously publishes last book. Imagine how many fun *BITS* he had in there.

I'll assume that you can imagine characters taking over the writing to develop themselves, if you accept this: writers distill facts into slivers of nuance to make characters read so real that the *BITS* of our own or others' lives are seen as only layers of fictional people. But... we live in fear that someone will recognize the source of one of our *BITS* in a real person and see the book as being all about him or her. That, I assure you, is what fiction writers see as a true horror story.

My latest project is a group of short stories that I hope readers come to see are parts of a novel I'll call *Surreptitious Glances*. Each is a few pages' glimpse at the lives of Helen, a woman of 50-ish, and Nick, her 25 year-old lover. I use that quaint term because this isn't a cougar's tale, nor about casual hook-ups; these two were friends whose warmth and trust led them to bed. Often, I think, but I still have gaps to fill in the tale, so I don't know how lucky they get. In that regard, fiction is a lot like life.

As there's some of the young me in Nick, and *BITS* of all the women I've ever loved in Helen, both write themselves. Just as athletes train to play the sport with what coaches call muscle memory, my mental muscle instinctively adds *BITS* of my experiences so characters show psychological integrity in credible responses to plot events. I live in hope that no *BIT* is so obvious it distracts from my fiction's themes.

But Helen and Nick needed backstories to evolve for readers, so I made her recently widowed, gave him a dysfunctional home life, and gave both families and friends. A free-spirited woman of Nick's age brings a playfully sexy relationship that restores him after some confidence-crushing affairs made him self-protective. When Helen enters his life, Nick is able to offer her the admirable man he has become because a wonderful woman has helped him to be that.

That *BIT* gave me only vague ideas for actions to take my tale to a credible end. But last night, while I was gazing at the ceiling, I reviewed a dream I'd had. Picture this, as Joe Heller gave us Rembrandt saying...

I was at a party, where people with intelligent faces commented, ostensibly wittily, on all that masquerades as life while sipping wine. As an outsider in their midst, I sat alone, watching them from some low seat, perhaps a footrest, as an oddly friendly cat took refuge from spilling drinks under my legs, which it then purringly molested. A louder sound of a familiar woman's voice instantly got me turning to look up.

There stood an ex-lover, an extraordinary woman I'd lost years ago. I was struck mute, recalling myriad scenes of us together as I gazed into her eyes as if they were windows to my memories. I could see our times glittering with splendidly laughter-adorned sex, and saw the care we shared in times of stress or ill health. As importantly, in my dream I felt the contentment I'd known as a façade-stripped me with her. But then I had to confront having seen her eyes change over time from care-free to ecstasy, then to despair; I wasn't proud of causing it. Still, she had been a force in my evolution to a man that others can now admire, respect, and even praise, and I've always known that none of it could have happened without her.

I heard concern creaking below her sociable tone as she asked: "Where's the you I knew – the old life of the party? Why don't you answer? You must know I still care about you. Are you all right? Please say you are."

All I said to her in my dream was: "I am now."

However, to the moonlight's reflected shimmer on my bedroom ceiling, I said: "Now I know that my story ends with them reuniting as loving friends, and proud to be that."

MINDFUL ACKNOWLEDGEMENTS...

Eternal gratitude goes to three wondrous women who shaped my life: ex-wives Larissa and Carolyn, now loving friends, and my partner of nine years, Pami, all of whom patiently helped me. They also encouraged me to free my mind of its many invaders by writing the characters' stories – then assessed my efforts honestly. To all past and present members of North Fork Writers Group go thanks for years of supportive camaraderie, but especially for all of their insightful suggestions for projects I shared with them. Extra thanks to volunteer proof-readers Helene Munson and Kit Storjohann, and also to Jean Schweibish for the flattering cover photo that Patty Hocker's graphic artistry adorned with text. Big thanks must to Shirrel Rhoades for his publishing patronage of short fiction for we who have irresistible urges to try to write mind-engaging entertainment.

In short... To all who have encouraged and guided me, I offer my heart-felt thanks.

- Dave P.

ABOUT … *J. David Porteous*

J is for James, but I was called Dave until USA dual citizenship exposed me to bureaucracies that cannot abide people who never use their first names – I'm still Dave to you. My Australian marketing & advertising career led me to start *Orchestrated Chaos,* a marketing communications company where I wrote for all media. That work earned me membership of the Australian Writers Guild decades ago, but for almost all of my life I have been writing stories and poems.

Since moving to the USA, work culminated in my research & writing company, *Hunt & Peck.* In recent years, as a member of the *North Fork Writers Group,* I offered four tales in our book, *7 VOICES* (The New Alantean Library, 2015). *STRANGERS IN MY MIND* is the first publication of exclusively my short fiction – more, and novels, are in the works.

I live in eastern Long Island with Pami and our dog Scruffy, enjoying a world of mind-stirring mates via the Internet, and all of my local friends, writers and artists in our North Fork area's creative community.

Courtesy of Bruce MacDonald, PhD, MFA, MSc...

THE NAME PORTEOUS

This Greek name (variables end *eus, ous, ius* or *us*) appears in pre-Christian Roman records, but is notable as Roman Army officers of that name were garrisoned at Hadrian's Wall on Scotland's border. As is evident in the Porteous Clan's split from Clan MacDonald, those Porteous lads had dallied with MacDonald lassies. Clan Porteous lived near the picturesque Tweed River, and the oldest known Porteous abode, a 14th century castle, was at Tweedsmuir, half-way between Edinburgh and Glasgow. The International Porteous Associates group erected a cairn comprised of the old castle's foundation stones to mark the site.

We Scots pronounce the name as *Por-chus*, and its original family trees' branches have held royalty, rebels and rustlers. Grandparents of this book's author, Alex (Free Kirk/Presbyterian) and Annie (Catholic-convert) fled from religious prejudice, hoping to reach the USA. Unable to get passage on the first ship departing from the U.K. (reputedly *The Titanic*) they went to Australia instead.
-- *BMcD*.

The New
Atlantian Library

NewAtlantianLibrary.com
or AbsolutelyAmazingEbooks.com
or AA-eBooks.com

www.ingramcontent.com/pod-product-compliance
Lightning Source LLC
Chambersburg PA
CBHW050401030726
47503CB00006B/1971